SWEETNESS

TORGNY LINDGREN was born in Norsjö, Sweden, in 1938. He is the prize-winning author of novels, poems and short stories. His works so far published in English include his novels *Bathsheba*, *The Way of a Serpent*, *Light*, and *In Praise of Truth*, and a collection of short stories, *Merab's Beauty*. His work is translated into 25 languages.

TOM GEDDES has regularly been Torgny Lindgren's English translator. His translation of *The Way of a Serpent* was awarded the Bernard Shaw Prize. His recent translations from the Swedish include Björn Larsson's *Long John Silver*.

Torgny Lindgren

SWEETNESS

Translated from the Swedish by
Tom Geddes

THE HARVILL PRESS
LONDON

First published in Sweden with the title *Hummelhonung*
by Norstedts Förlag AB, Stockholm, 1995

First published in Great Britain in 2000 by
The Harvill Press,
2 Aztec Row, Berners Road,
London N1 0PW

www.harvill.com

1 3 5 7 9 8 6 4 2

A CIP catalogue record for this book
is available from the British Library

The Publishers gratefully acknowledge the
financial support of the Swedish Institute
towards the publication of this book in English

ISBN 1 86046 656 7

Designed and typeset in Quadraat
at Libanus Press, Marlborough, Wiltshire

Printed and bound in Great Britain by Butler & Tanner Ltd
at Selwood Printing, Burgess Hill

SWEETNESS

AFTER THE LECTURE SHE was going to stay at a little guest-house, and would be moving on the next day. She had her clothes in the big bag with the shoulder-strap, and all her personal effects in her briefcase: books, writing pad and pens.

When the audience had taken their seats in the village hall, all fifteen of them, an old blind woman was wheeled up to the empty floor-space below the rostrum. Her eyes were open and covered in a grey film, with no pupil and no iris. It was to the blind woman that she chose to address herself, to her worn and weathered little face.

The girl who had pushed the wheelchair in sat down too, and was reading a comic that she propped up against the blind woman's shoulder.

Holy fools.

Some of them are called saints, she said, but there are no common characteristics; the designation is ascribed to them by chance or by circumstance; if anything, they can be characterised by an impassioned or tormented awareness of existence, an almost morbid intensification of hearing and alertness yet at the same time an unworldly detachment in everyday life.

Some of them seem to have loved their fellow human beings, others not.

The audience sat there in their overcoats, smelling of damp wool. They had seen the little item about her lecture in the newspaper. They might have also seen the stencilled poster on the noticeboard outside or in the local Co-op. If I don't go, they had thought, there'll be no one there.

They sat completely motionless; the only person who made an occasional movement was the girl behind the wheelchair, turning the pages of her comic.

St Ethelreda went through two marriages intact, her absent-mindedness keeping her from the ultimate union; a concentrated, almost convulsive distraction holding its hand over her virginity. When St Methodius was executed he seemed hardly to notice, his decapitated head continuing to preach to the assembled heathens – on the resurrection of the body and on free will.

And so forth.

She had once written a book on Johan Axel Samuelsson, the felon who murdered the Mobergs, the vicar and his wife in Tillberga. He had wanted to live in imitation of Christ, but lacked the aptitude. That winter she had travelled from place to place lecturing on the lives of criminals, her talks paid for by cultural foundations and educational associations and lecture societies.

She obviously knew her text by heart. As she spoke her hand played incessantly with the buttons on her thick green and white striped cardigan. From time to time she put her thumb up to her right eye, probably to control some kind of nervous tic.

Over by the door a man sat fast asleep, his head fallen

forward on to his chest, the pendants of the seven-branched chandelier on the ceiling reflecting on his shiny bald pate. He seemed not to be breathing, except for a sigh now and then, either of devout respect or in order not to suffocate.

She usually spoke for fifty minutes, or forty-five if for some incomprehensible reason her enthusiasm was aroused.

Even in this life holy men, or those so described, are imbued with an awareness that they represent, that they stand for something nameless and distinct from their own selves, rather than living in the usual sense; that their world is a world of representation, that in a dog-like way they are imitating their master. No, imitate is not the right word: in their own lives they incorporate an unknown life; they are metaphorically related to someone or something they do not know but would like to know. And even in this pale and shadowy form they contain a drop of that alien life; despite withered flesh and worn nails they are still a mixture of memory and desire.

They continued listening even after she had finished speaking. Why should they understand her? Without asking any questions, without so much as a glance of gratitude or empathy, one by one they got up and left. The girl with the comic wheeled the blind woman out.

Only the man who had been asleep remained where he was, fully awake now.

"I'm the person you're staying with," he said.

She did not seem surprised. Cheap accommodation, that was how the organisers saved money. She picked up her coat and bags and walked over to him.

They looked at one another.

He was wearing a filthy black leather jacket over a check shirt and woollen pullover. The skin drooped slackly on his face; he had obviously been quite a big man once, but all his bulk had been eaten away from within by unknown forces. He smelled of putrefaction.

She was a single woman in her forty-fifth year, a stranger from the south who had written books about love and death and saints, books that hardly anyone bothered to read; a speaker with a voice of such a mournful, shrill and monotonous quality that it could never convince anyone of anything. In outward appearance she was thin, sharp and self-contained.

"You drive," he said, handing her his car key, which was tied to a shapeless piece of wood, black with grime and grease. When he stood up he tottered, and walked with knees bent and a waddling motion, as though he were carrying an enormous burden on his shoulders. His clothes hung limp and loose on his skinny body, as if borrowed from someone else, a giant.

He confided his name to her: Hadar. And she told him hers, despite the fact that he presumably knew it.

The car was parked outside the door.

"It's not very far," he said. "Ten miles or so."

And he went on to ask, "Can you drive?"

"Yes," she said. "I can drive."

She drove without any show of of interest, as if indifferent. His car was old and dented and flaking with rust. He did not need to tell her the way: there was only one road.

Although it was already dark, the sky in the west still

6

glowed yellow above the treetops. It was the twentieth of October, and there were patches of snow by the roadside.

"All landscapes and all the roads that wend their way across them have their own individual character and quality," she said, as if talking to herself. "They all have their drawbacks and imperfections.

"This road is very straight and narrow, over a terrain of scrub."

"I shall never drive again now," he said. "Coming here was my last time."

Though he did not say it quite like that. His speech was a northern dialect with grotesquely lengthened vowels and dark, gloomy diphthongs; what she heard was a translation of the kind that visitors always imagine they hear in foreign countries.

"I read about you in the paper," he said. "You could have been sent by God. We've never had anyone like you hereabouts before. Not that there is a God. Nor any mercy either. But even so."

She opened the window a chink. His smell was penetrating her nostrils and sinuses and clinging to the pores of her face and hands.

"How could God have sent me if He doesn't exist?" she asked. "And why should He have sent me?"

"He knows about you. He's heard about you. Because of all those holy people you go around giving talks about. He reads the North Västerbothnian."

From time to time he raised his hand and pointed towards the beam of the headlights in front of the windscreen, as if he were trying to say 'This is the way, along here!'

"It's just how things worked out," she said. "I wrote a book

7

on holy fools, with nothing special in mind. You can write books on anything.

"And I'm giving up lecturing," she went on. "This was the last. I'm going away somewhere tomorrow, early tomorrow morning, anywhere."

When he turned towards her and breathed over her she gave a start as if she found it particularly offensive. It was really extraordinary that a person could smell like that.

The road was climbing steadily, and the countryside was becoming whiter.

"There used to be some things I believed in," he said. "But in the end you can't see any further than the hand in front of your face. Everything disintegrates and falls apart. I've got cancer and will die soon.

"But," he added, "I'm in no hurry. We shouldn't be too eager."

She did not attempt to refute his claim that he was dying. It was altogether too obvious. He should have been dead long ago.

They met no other cars, and there was no sign of any houses with lights in their windows.

He probably had a housekeeper or a wife waiting for them, who would have made up a bed for the speaker in the living room, a folding bed with a lumpy, flattened mattress. And put out some old dry rye bread and butter and cheese on the table.

He leant forward and turned his face towards her, lifting the earflaps on his check peaked cap, as if he were expecting an answer. Perhaps he wanted her to comment on the fact that he was dying.

"Is it much further?" she asked. "Are we nearly there?"

"We've just passed Frans Lindgren's peat bogs. So that's where we've got to."

He went on gazing at her, not seeming to notice that it was dark, almost pitch black, inside the car, as if willing her to speak to him. She slowed down a little and gave him her views on conversation, what she thought about conversation in general terms.

She had never found conversation appealing or enticing. In conversation thoughts are always being forced into unpredictable feints or digressions, they are twisted and distorted to please or annoy, they can be villainously treacherous. Solitary thought, on the other hand, is sovereign, it stays confined within and doesn't have to make compromises. Even when you're in two minds you remain whole. She wanted to be left in peace with her thoughts. But in fact she was not all that keen on thinking. Thoughts were corrosive.

And, she went on, if she had anything to say she would usually make a note of it and put it in her books or refer to it in her lectures.

The engine gave a cough now and then, but she seemed not to notice. And he was probably used to it.

"I must have a pee," he said.

She pulled in and came to a halt at the side of the road. He opened the door, swung round and, placing his feet on the snowy verge, passed water from a half-sitting position. Possibly in order to avoid hearing the splash of urine against the side of the car she decided to say something.

"Saints are by definition dead," she explained, "and that's why I've chosen to write about them; they can't dissimulate any more, all that's left of them is individual bones. When you write about them you hardly need to know anything, really. They're just ordinary people, although of course also touched by genius."

And about death she had this to say:

"My parents died in a plane crash, when I was eight. Since then no one has died as far as I'm concerned. My idea of death is of falling. When we die, then immediately we have always been dead. Or something along those lines."

When he had finished peeing she drove on.

At the top of a hill, where a cart stood upended to mark the bank of a ditch, she had to turn off to the right, on to a road that had not been snowploughed. The only indications that it was a road were the wheel tracks in the snow.

In the morning, she told him, she would take a bus south, to one of the small towns out on the coast; she would rent a room on the upper floor of a yellow wooden house, preferably with a sullen, short-sighted widow who could make tea and bake scones for her. There, on a heavy oak desk from the forties, she would write a book about St Christopher. Then she would be finished with these holy men for ever, finished with miracles and superhuman compassion and heavenly visions.

He started speaking again, and she translated to herself, muttering it under her breath as she did so:

"This is the most beautiful landscape on earth. No one ought to have to die here. You can stretch out your hand anywhere in this part of the country and always find yourself pointing at a wonder of nature, whether you want to or not, a sight or a miracle that far surpasses your understanding. I've never seen any other region myself, never felt the need.

"It's a landscape for connoisseurs of snow and ice and hoar-frost, and also for lovers of ancient spruce, birch scrub, scattered stones, waterlogged marshes and cold springs. And ermine – which only show themselves to us humans when we are about to die, anyway.

"This was where I was conceived, beneath a pile of hay-rack poles; my father showed me the place. Fifteen-foot poles! And eleven-foot cross-pieces, imagine that! That's what you ought to write about!

"If it weren't for the law – laws come from the south and they're quite perverse – then my final wish would be to be buried here on the edge of a marsh under a giant fir with a magpie's nest in its crown!"

The road continued relentlessly upwards; she drove in second gear. He blew his nose into the palm of his hand and wiped it meticulously on his trousers.

And at last a pair of illumined windows came into view. "There!" he said. "We're here! Already!"

He opened the door and let her into the house. He was panting for breath from climbing the three steps and he turned the key in the lock with a groan, his lungs emitting a dull rattle as he said, "Now you can see a real house, a house a person can live in!"

He did not even give himself time to sit down, but straight-away showed her round: kitchen, bedroom, living room. Stick-back chairs, wash-stand, drop-leaf table, sofa bed, wall-hangings, pedestal table. And the table zither.

"Mother," he said. "She used to play 'By the Shore of Lake Roine'. It's by Topelius."

In the kitchen three big branches were fixed to the wall

by the stove, looking like lopped-off misshapen bows.

"What's that?" she asked.

"Oh, that's just a contraption," he said. "A special contraption."

He went ahead of her up the stairs to the attic, stopping half way to rest, supporting himself with his hands on his knees.

"This is where you'll sleep," he said.

"Anywhere will do," she said. "It's only for one night."

It was a small mansard room with a single window. There was a white crocheted bedspread on the bed, a little square table in front of the window, and a heavy armchair.

"There," he said, "you can sit and write there. About the man I've forgotten the name of."

"Christopher," she said. "St Christopher."

To which she added, "But I only write in the mornings. And I'll be leaving tomorrow morning."

"I made this room for my father," he said, "so that the old man would have somewhere to die."

"It's a nice little room," she said.

"Well, he thought it was a good place to die, anyway," said Hadar.

They ate supper in the kitchen, crispbread and boiled bacon. He showed her his painkillers and sleeping tablets as he pushed them into the butter under the meat. And she asked whether he lived alone, whether he had anyone to help him, whether there was anyone who came.

But he made no answer, saying instead, "Really and truly I can't eat bacon any more. But what's a man to do? What are we without meat? A life without meat, that's not a life fit for human beings. It's meat that keeps us upright. Without meat there would be no certainty in the world."

She had nothing to say about meat. Food, she said, had never been especially important to her.

"But this tastes good," she said.

"Ah!" he said. "Bacon!"

As he spoke he took the morsel he was chewing out of his mouth and held it in his hand; then he stuffed it back in again. And then, while he was still chewing, he started undoing the buttons on his shirt and undressing for the night.

Before going to bed in the attic she opened the window for a while, to clear the air of his smell. And she laid out her books and writing pad on the little table. It looked as if it were a habit, as if she always did it, wherever she spent the night. The writing pad was her home; in all probability she wrote constantly in her thoughts.

His real name was not Christopher but Offerus or possibly Reprobus; he was of Canaanite extraction and twelve spans tall. The object of his existence, the mission which he himself had selected or which nature with her uncompromising discipline had invested in his character, was to serve, a service which implied above all a state of being chosen and consecrated, not subservience; a service so exquisite and magnificent that he would never more need or be able to bring himself to ask the meaning of life; a service that comprised at one and the same time ultimate sacrifice and utter exhaustion and absolute satisfaction. Over his shoulders he wore eight goatskins sewn together, around his hips the hide of an ass, and his beard covered his chest. He had a bald pate, but two dark curly tufts of hair over his ears. He was wont to spit and say "Devil take it! Devil take it!" In some pictures he carries a knotted staff in his hand, in others his empty, tightly clenched fists are held close to his chest. His forehead and cheeks are running in sweat.

Before she fell asleep she also scribbled a note to her publisher: she had had her lecture fee sent to them; the freezing cold was terrible in this godforsaken back of beyond; she was content, in fact getting on well; she would have a manuscript ready by the spring. St Christopher, the Holy Bearer of all Burdens. "I'll post this letter in the morning when I get back to the village," she wrote.

When she came down to the kitchen again in the morning, woken by the unnatural silence, he was already dressed and lying on the sofa with his hands clasped over his shrunken belly.

It had been snowing. Through the window she could see her surroundings for the first time: the long, bare hillside, the pine forest, a flat surface that might be a lake, the ridge of the mountains. It was a landscape in which the morning light had all the space it needed. And the snow lay thick over the whole of this immense, paralysed desolation.

"How am I going to get away now?" she asked.

"The mornings are the worst," he said. "Before the tablets take effect. Then you just have to lie in fear and trembling up here in Övreberg."

She did not ask what he was in fear of, but repeated, "How am I going to get away?"

"You won't get away," he said. "There won't be a snow-plough here for several days. You might just as well . . ."

She noticed now that there was a house lower down the hill. She could not actually see it; it was the smoke from its chimney that was visible.

"So you've got neighbours," she said. "You're not entirely on your own in Övreberg."

"It's not neighbours," he said. "No – no neighbours."

"But I can see the house," she said. "There's smoke coming from the chimney."

"Yes," he said. "There's always smoke, right enough. It's a sign that he's alive."

"Who?" she asked. "Who is it that's alive?"

"My brother. Olof. If it weren't for him, I'd have been dead long ago."

She glanced round at him quickly. What did he look like when he actually uttered a few words that on the face of it were full of warmth?

"I'm not going to make that bastard happy by dying before him," he went on. "That's what keeps me alive, and I'll never let him get the upper hand."

There was really quite a lot of smoke pouring out of the chimney down there, black smoke rising defiantly against the blinding white snow.

"I've got cancer and he's got his heart. Cancer is said to be worse, but the heart is like a mushroom, it can collapse in a second. So he shouldn't take anything for granted. The bastard."

Never before had she seen anything like this covering of snow that levelled everything, this – as she also said to him – interminable feather bed, this lather of light transformed into matter. Perhaps she should write a few lines about the landscape of legend, the landscape in which nearly all the saints had lived, where Christopher travelled round with his staff, a landscape devoid of almost every feature.

"When will the roads be cleared?" she asked.

"You can never tell," he replied. "They send the snow-plough when they've got time. And no one can pretend that it's particularly urgent out here."

THEY ATE BREAKFAST. It consisted of exactly the same as the meal the previous evening. "I eat so little and so slowly now," he said. "Everything about me has shrunk, my chest, my skull, my jaws, my throat."

Then he lay down on the sofa again.

And she went outside. Someone ought to shovel away some of that frightful snow.

A cat crept in past her feet.

"Well, you've got a cat, anyway," she said.

"I've always had her," he replied. "She's called Minna. She usually sleeps in the crook of my knees. She pees in that fur hat outside the door. I'll probably put her down."

There, sure enough, was a fur hat turned inside-out, reeking pungently of urine. It was quite large; he must have had it before his head started to shrink.

A shovel too stood leaning against the wall by the door; he had known the snow was on its way.

She cleared the steps, and dug out a semi-circle in front of the house and a narrow path to the barn. The snow came up over her knees.

In the landscape of legend, she would write that evening, the mountain is the Mountain, the river the River, the forest the Forest and the sea the Sea. The particular is always the universal, the individual element of the landscape represents the essence of the phenomenon and therefore appears to lack the individuality that all phenomena normally exhibit in nature. The world is levelled out, transformed into a bloodless abstraction, it invites indifference, not to say dissociation. The figures of legend imbue their surroundings with their representative quality, and the landscape itself becomes representative.

When she came back in, he said, "Ah yes, it was certainly a good thing that you turned up just in time to shovel the snow for me."

She sat down by the window and looked out at the snowdrifts below the house and at the mountains over on the horizon. In appearance they were exactly the same, the snowdrifts and the mountains. He lay still with his eyes closed, perhaps asleep. The clock on the wall ticked away, wheezing into life now and then to strike the hours and half hours.

But he was not asleep, and suddenly asked, "Is there still smoke coming from Olof's house?"

"Yes, there's smoke."

The cat was lying on his chest. It certainly looked ancient, its hind legs almost bald, its whiskers, cheeks and ears faded and yellowing.

He opened his eyes and raised his head slightly so that he could see her.

"Perhaps you could get some food out and put it on the table," he said.

"Are you hungry?" she asked.

No, nowadays he could never enjoy a proper feeling of hunger. "But you must be hungry," he said.

"Yes," she said. "Perhaps I am."

She asked what food she should get.

He pointed towards the door. She should just go out there, out to the cow shed; there was everything you could think of out there, in fact he couldn't help chuckling gently to himself as he said it.

"There's food there all right!"

The long barn that was built on to the cow shed was full of wood, chopped and split birch wood, heaped up from floor to ceiling. And inside the cow shed she found similar piles: sacks of flour and grain, packs of butter and sugar and macaroni, mountains of crispbread and tinned food and cheeses and boxes of dried fish and two barrels of Iceland herring. From the ceiling hung sausages and smoked shoulders and legs of ham. And a carcass of dried mutton.

She picked out a can of stew. Food to guarantee survival, it said on the label. In the mountains, in the forests, at sea.

"You look as if you're prepared for war," she said as she came back in.

"It is war," he replied.

She seemed to have become accustomed to his smell; she was completely at ease as she ate. He was having to force his food slowly and with some difficulty down his shrunken throat.

He even paused briefly in his chewing to say, "There's nothing wrong with my teeth."

And he raised his upper lip with his thumb and showed her: they were blunted and worn down, but strong, with none missing.

"Though it's a shame to have teeth like this," he continued, "when I'm dying of cancer and they'll be wasted."

"Yes," she replied. "Those teeth could last for years yet."

He had a lot more to say about the body; the act of eating and the stew made him think about it seriously for a moment. She sat opposite him interpreting and summarising for herself what he was saying.

It was the most natural thing in the world, the body. It was there, carrying out its functions, even if you didn't give it a single thought. It was a harmonious conjunction of mobile and rigid elements, of fluid and solid, mucus and enamel; it seemed to be a cleverly, even skilfully designed composite of parts which, viewed separately, might appear ridiculous or in certain instances even repulsive. But the sum total, the body as a structured, complex contraption, deserved both respect and admiration; in fact you could even imagine that it was permanently in need of such respect and admiration. It had no counterpart, it was completely unique in the whole world. As a species, it had relatives, of course, but as an individual, as a particular body, it was totally alone, left to its fate and exposed to outside forces. So it made its most profound and crucial bonds and connections inwards into itself, combinations and lines of communication that the body's lord and master would as a general rule only perceive in the form of confused behaviour patterns or, at worst, disturbing manifestations of illness. At one time in the past he had had a woman – he would give her a more detailed account on a future occasion, if she would permit him to – and in the intoxication of love his body had started to lose its hair. His body had construed love to mean that it should shed everything; his hair loss had had a symbolic function, so to speak. After that unpleasant experience he had regarded his body with some suspicion. And he felt quite alarmed: he would really rather keep all his bodily parts until he died, he didn't want to lose an occasional tooth or a finger here and a toe there. Only entire and unscathed could a person – in other words, the body – retain his pride and equilibrium and dignity.

"Would you mind bringing in the wood when we've finished eating?" he added.

So, after she had done the washing-up, she brought in some wood. She carried it in the wicker basket that was standing by the kitchen stove. She stopped at the foot of the steps for a few moments to listen: a snowplough should be audible from a good distance, and when it came she would pick up her bags and trudge out to the main road. A passing car would surely take pity on her. The snowplough would come like an emissary from civilisation, a link to culture and society. Perhaps there might even be room for her and her small amount of luggage in the snowplough itself, in the driver's cab.

She brought three baskets of wood indoors and stacked it by the stove. At least he wouldn't freeze; he was going to have to manage until someone came to help him.

"But I've cut down on a lot of things," he said. "I've cut down on almost everything. I've only got absolute necessities in the barn."

He had reverted to her observation that he seemed to have prepared for a state of war. He was standing at the kitchen window, gazing out towards his brother's house.

He had gathered in all the loose threads that had still been trailing from his life, he had pruned and cast off everything that was not essential, and had kept only what was fundamental and indispensable. He felt able to claim that he now had nothing left, over and above naked existence itself. Cancer and himself, that ought to suffice.

"When you have so little life left," he said, "it shouldn't be extravagant."

And he gave her an account of the measures he had taken.

He had had the telephone disconnected. Who could he have brought himself to speak to in this condition, not to mention the various conditions that still lay ahead of him? He had informed the hospital and the authorities in the village that no one should come, no one should be put to the trouble of the journey; he didn't have the strength to receive people, to be polite to nurses and home-helps and all the other kinds of carers, to make coffee for them and bake cakes. He had buried his television set in the potato patch: he had enough – more than enough – woes and afflictions of his own to worry about.

And he had written to his relations in Sundsvall and taken his leave of them, they weren't to go to the bother of sending him Christmas cards any more.

But he had kept the newspaper on. The newspaper would come after the snowplough had been. That was where he had found her, on the back page.

And the doctor had given him such quantities of painkillers that he would be able to suffer and die five or six times over without any difficulty.

But he wanted to make it clear that even such a restricted and diminished life had its own beauty, a pure and polished lustre, scarcely describable to an outsider, a radiance peculiar to the simple act of living itself. In this situation an almost morbid attention to the absolute essential, survival, was the decisive factor. No, survival was obviously the wrong word: the finite, provisional continuation of existence, the venture into the temporary prolongation of life. Because it was a hazardous venture, a stressful exercise that drew its distinctive intensity and astringency and freshness from the circumstance of his also having a fellow-competitor, or rather an opponent: his brother, Olof, who constantly reminded him with his smoke-signals that his heart had not yet ceased beating. In short: the fact that he was still alive himself was due to his battle against his own sickness and for his brother's; to his opposition to his brother's continued existence but his desire for his own.

"Come and look!" he said. "That smoke's damned thin, isn't it, the smoke from that chimney of his?"

"Yes," she said. "Or, more to the point, I can't see any smoke at all."

"Sometimes," he went on, "sometimes he plays tricks on me. He lets the stove nearly go out so that I'll think it's all over. But then he gets it going at full blast again."

"He probably has other things to do," she said. "He can't just sit by the stove tending the fire."

"Well, I don't know what else he could have to do."

"He must have to look after himself," she said. "And he has to take care of his illness. His heart."

"You should tend a fire regularly and carefully," said Hadar, "you have to feed a fire as if it were a new-born lamb."

And he felt he had to repeat it. The circumstances of a life should be adapted to suit the life itself: only grand lives can support grand circumstances. In a modest and humble existence you should tend a fire calmly and steadily and decently.

"Look!" she cried, "it's thickening up again. There! You'd never get smoke any thicker and blacker than that!"

"I must have something to do," she said.

"Sit down and write," said Hadar.

"If I go and sit down to write upstairs," she said, "the snowplough might come without my noticing it."

"Everything here's already done," he said.

"I can do anything. Anything at all – really."

She found a zinc bowl in a cupboard at the back of the kitchen. She heated the water in four saucepans on the stove, then she scrubbed the floor. And she told him she was going to wash his clothes. When the snowplough came and she went on her way he would be clean and largely free from his stench. It would be a good deed towards the next person who came, the one who would have to come to look after him.

"What shall I put on, then?" he asked. "What clothes shall I wear if you're washing these?"

"Put anything on," she said, "just while these are drying."

"I don't remember ever having any other clothes," he said. And he elaborated: Clothes were not just something incidental, they were not to be treated carelessly or arbitrarily, they belonged to a person in a deeply personal and fundamental way. She must understand that he had always had this red and blue check shirt, this woollen pullover and these black trousers; these clothes were the only right ones for him. Obviously generations of shirts, pullovers and trousers had succeeded one another, but in principle they had always been the same. In summer he usually did without the pullover, of course, but that was mainly to avoid the mosquitoes; gnats and mosquitoes were attracted to wool. And clothes should only be washed in moderation; water consumed the cloth and broke up the fibres, buttons worked loose and seams came apart. There was also a considerable risk that they would start to smell in a way that was alien to the body; the smell of water was cold and inhospitable, and after any such totally superfluous washing the body had to go to a lot of trouble to assert its dominance over the clothes again, as it were. He would even venture to suggest that moral decline and the increasing breakdown of society had their origin in this objectionable and exaggerated desire to wash everything. And you also had to think of the water: when one day all the water had been washed away, no one would be able to stop forest fires and desertification any more. That was all he wanted to say.

In the end, however, he handed over his clothes to her anyway, after she had heard him out. It was not modesty that inhibited him; he did not seem concerned about whether she might see him more or less naked – it was the clothes he did not wish to expose and surrender.

She washed and rinsed, washed and rinsed, and changed the water in the zinc bowl five times. When the last lot of water did not turn slimy, but just grey, she gave up. Whoever came afterwards to look after him properly could give them a more thorough and definitive wash.

She had hung the red and blue check and the black rags she had used for scrubbing on the damper above the stove, and now she put the clothes out to dry on the strange rough branches that were fixed to the wall on the left of the stove.

But that was something he could not allow under any circumstances. Certainly not, the special contraption was not to be used for things like that, household things, so to speak, that was not what it was intended for at all. No, she could put up a line somewhere, wherever she wanted, between two door-handles or between some of the bent nails knocked into the walls here and there. She only had herself to blame, he took no responsibility for this damned washing. She was from the south and always knew best, so she would find an answer. All he wanted to say was that he had expected more consideration and modest respect on her part right at the beginning of their relationship.

Perhaps there was only one snowplough in the whole of this desolate region. This one snowplough would be carving its relentless course along the straight narrow roads, across the bogs and through the pine forests; darkness was already falling and the light from its headlamps would be swallowed up by these endless wastes. It would be thundering on day and night without ever coming to a halt. This landscape could never be ploughed free of snow.

Hadar was lying on the sofa. "Is there a light on in Olof's house?" he asked. "Is there smoke coming out of the chimney?"

"No," she said, "there's no light and no smoke."

"You ought to write," he said. "You should be sitting up in your room writing. You should be writing books."

"It's not as easy as that," she replied. "It's not like eating and sleeping."

"You don't need to worry about me," he said. "I'll get by, I'll be all right."

The cat that had been lying at his feet was standing by the door again, so she let it out. "It'll freeze to death out there," she said. She switched on the light.

"The idea is that you should sit up in the bedroom and have some peace and quiet," he said. "Now that you've taken refuge here. You can sit up there with your pen in your hand and concentrate on your thoughts.

"That's the idea," he reiterated.

And then he asked again about his neighbour's smoke and light.

"No," she said, "it's completely dark and still."

At that he raised his head from the cushion, even got himself into a half-sitting position by supporting himself on both elbows, and had to gasp for breath for a moment before he could say, "Maybe something has happened to him!"

"He might have gone out somewhere," she said.

"He's at home," said Hadar. "He hasn't got anywhere else he could be; even if he's dead, he's at home."

"Is there anyone to keep an eye on him?"

"Who would want to keep an eye on him?" said Hadar. "A man like him! No, no decent and honest person would want anything to do with him!"

There was a thermometer hanging on two rusty nails outside the window.

"It's nearly minus five," she said. "He ought to have his stove on. I presume there's no limit to how cold it can get up here."

He could confirm that: the cold had no limits. The birds could fall out of the trees, their legs frozen stiff; the lakes could freeze to the bottom no matter how deep they were; your breath would no longer form vapour but icicles.

"But at present," he said, "at present it's still only autumn."

"There are birds here in winter, then?" she asked.

"Good heavens, yes! Thousands of birds, flocks as well as the poor solitary devils!" He was more than willing to list them for her: sparrows, capercaillie, yellowhammers, wagtails, bullfinches, ptarmigan, fieldfares, waxwings, black grouse – both the cock and the hen – woodpeckers, hawks, hazel-grouse. And cranes.

"I can't believe it," she said. "Not cranes."

"Well, I can't be expected to know everything," he said. "You're asking the impossible of me. I can't keep tabs on every bird!"

The newly washed clothes and the scrubbed floor were beginning to steam up the window panes, and she wiped off the mist with her sleeve. He had lain down again.

"He must have put his light on by now," he said. "You have to put the light on so that you don't stumble over a chair or your boots in the dark and fall on the stove and set yourself on fire."

"No, the windows are in darkness, I can hardly see the house any more."

He was silent for a long time. When he eventually spoke he looked at her with wide-open eyes. "I suppose nothing has happened to him. He might be lying dead over there. At last. The bastard. Though what if he's only half dead? We don't want him to have to suffer. The swine. Any more than necessary."

"If only the snowplough would come," she said, "then he'd be able to get some help."

"Ah," he said, "you can have faith in the snowplough. You being from the south."

"If he really is dead," she said, "then he won't be needing either fire or light."

"Somebody at least should go and take a look at him," said Hadar. "If there were anyone who could bring themselves to. If anyone knew about him. If he weren't so disgusting. But as it is he'll just have to lie there."

"It's nothing to do with me," she said. "I don't know him."

Hadar said nothing for a while.

"I hadn't thought of that," he said. "But it's true. You don't know him. You've never even heard him spoken of. As far as you're concerned he could be just anybody. So that's that."

She had to wade and trudge through the snow down to the house. Someone should have cleared the path: there must presumably have been one between the brothers' houses.

She knocked on the door several times, but inside there was silence. So she went in, through the little hall that led into the kitchen, and turned on the light switch to the right of the door, in exactly the same place as in Hadar's house.

The switch and the bare bulb suspended from the ceiling were not the only things that made this kitchen an exact replica of his brother's. The sofa, the table and chairs, the stove, the worn wooden floor, the wall clock, everything looked the same as Hadar's. The only things missing were the rough branches on the wall, the special contraption. And the stove: this one was the old black kind.

He was lying on the sofa, the brother, Olof, the man with the weak heart. He had his hands clasped over his huge stomach, the cloth of his trousers had split open in several places so that his white flesh was protruding, and heavy rolls of fat on his cheeks and neck, almost like a pouch, hung down on to the cushion. His eyes were not visible in his swollen face, but he seemed to be turning them towards her.

"Ah," he said, "that was what I thought. That you would come. I've been lying here waiting for you."

And he asked who she was.

"You say you've been waiting for me," she said. "Yet you ask me who I am."

"I knew he'd got himself somebody," he said. "Hadar. I've been expecting it for a long time."

"He's worried about you," she said. "He asked me to come over. He wanted to know whether you were still alive."

"If he's worried about me," said Olof, "I'll never forgive him."

And he went on, "He's never been man enough to look after himself, has Hadar. He's always just taken what he wanted. In every way."

A bowl of sugar lumps stood on the chair by the sofa; he evidently needed one constantly in his mouth.

"That was what I thought," he said. "I thought that if I didn't set the fire in the stove and turn on the light, he would send you over. Then I'd see who it was, that was the idea. The person he's got for himself."

"When the road has been cleared," she said, "I'll be on my way. I'm waiting for the snowplough."

She stood over by the door looking at him. His corpulence was really extraordinary. But he was obviously dying.

Only now did she notice the cat. It had jumped on to the sofa and curled up at his feet.

"It must have come with me," she said. "And slunk in at the door without my seeing it. Minna. Hadar's cat."

He put a sugar lump in his mouth, but did not chew it; he probably had no teeth.

"So," he said. "So, he says the cat is his. Leo. He's been my cat for twelve years. He's a tom and his name's Leo. He'll outlive me."

She sat down on one of the chairs at the table. She might just as well sit here for a while as with his brother. Olof's smell was not as nauseating and repugnant as Hadar's. Before she went she would take a look at the cat. It was odd that this decrepit animal had the strength and capacity to belong to both of them, female with one and male with the other.

"And what do you do apart from this?" he asked. "When you're not with that old corpse?"

"Your brother?" she said. "You mean Hadar?"

Unopened bags of sugar were stacked up on the floor by the bedroom door. There were about a dozen boxes of chocolates at the end of the sofa, and under the table packs of raisins lay in a heap. Sweetmeats of every variety were spread all over the kitchen: on the window sills, in the metal buckets by the outside door, beneath the sofa, by the sink. Packets of sweets, tins of syrup, granulated sugar, honey, cartons of lozenges.

He must have seen her looking round, and he clearly felt obliged to give her an explanation.

"I thrive on sweet things," he said, "they give me nourishment."

He continued with an explanatory eulogy to sweetness, a solemn glorification which she attentively translated to herself; it was hard to make out what was her murmuring and what was his speech.

He owed it to this sweet nourishment that he was still alive, that despite his pitiful state he still had such incredible strength and stamina. A body such as his was appallingly heavy to bear, like a barrel of salt pork. Only sweet things provided the necessary nourishment; without the energy that sweet things contained he would be lying there like a beached whale. If he filled his mouth with raisins and sugar, it gave him the strength to switch on the light and carry in the wood and set a fire in the stove, for as long as the mouthful lasted, at any rate. Sweetness permeated your whole being. It was not just the bright red taste on your tongue and palate – no, it even tickled your earlobes and moistened and refreshed your toenails; it was an antidote to all the bitterness and gall in this harsh existence, it smoothed out the troughs and peaks between fear and hope, it created equanimity. Yes, to tell the truth, this phenomenon called happiness was in reality nothing other than sweetness: the experience of sweetness and happiness were one and the same thing.

And the older you got, the more you learnt about life, the deeper and more varied the quality of sweetness became; there was a development of sweetness in us, a constant increase in the possibilities and effects of sweetness. He occasionally imagined, he said, that there was something he had not yet tasted, a perfect sweetmeat, he imagined that everything he had tried up to now had just given him a foretaste; he thought that honey and barley sugar and chocolate were just pointers to something that was so sweet that it was beyond description.

His voice was squeaky and he was uttering his words staccato fashion, as if the rapid beating of his heart were affecting his speech. He probably would have liked to say even more about sweetness.

"But for everyday life," he said, "it's just for the warmth;

the sugar lumps keep me warm – you can see I'm sweating even though there's no fire in the stove."

He really did have beads of sweat on his brow.

"I'll light the fire," she said.

She owed him an answer now to the question of what she did otherwise, what she did when she was not with Hadar. "I write books," she said. "I'm about to write a book on St Christopher."

"Who is St Christopher?" he asked.

She stuffed twigs and birch-bark into the stove as she tried to answer that question too. The fire caught almost immediately. There were no books on St Christopher, she said, and she intended to bring together the plethora of anecdotes and scraps and fragments and legends into one whole. It was not possible to give a clear and unambiguous account of who he might have been. She would write down the ideas that came to her. She just wanted to do her best so that there would actually be a book about St Christopher.

The cat was still lying at his feet. Before she left he said to her, "Yes, the stove has to be lit so that the wall clock doesn't get cold and stop. If the clock stops, then you never know."

Hadar was standing at the window in his nightshirt, leaning against the sill. The effort of standing upright was making his legs and the flannel fabric quiver and shake.

"You've been a long time," he said. "The idea wasn't that you should stay down there and look after him."

"He's ill," she said. "He ought to have somebody to help him."

"He's not as ill as he ought to be," said Hadar. "He should have been dead long ago."

He carried on peering out of the window, out into the evening darkness. His legs might give way at any moment, and he would not have the strength to pull himself up if he fell. She put her arm round his waist and took hold of his wrists and helped him back to the sofa. He lay there panting for a long time, and she put wood in the stove and laid out bread and butter on the table.

"Is he eating sugar?" he asked. "Is that still his only sustenance, sugar?"

"Sugar lumps," she replied, "and honey and chocolate and raisins and peppermint rock and toffees and brown sugar. It'll be the death of him."

She went on to add that it was this that would be the decisive factor in their duel, if it really was a duel. Olof, his brother, was shortening his life by several days for every sugar lump and toffee and bar of chocolate he ate; and she listed what would undoubtedly follow: inflammation not only of the pancreas but of the bile-duct and the blood vessels of the head, thrombosis, heart attacks, bedsores, cerebral haemorrhages.

"It's not that simple," said Hadar. "He's still got the sugar to live for. If only I had something like his sugar."

Then she thought of the cat, and opened the door to let it in, in case it was standing outside in the cold. But there was no cat there.

She tried mentioning the snowplough again. "I'm sure," she said, "that once the road has been cleared they'll come to fetch you both. In an ambulance. Hospital, one of the hospitals on the coast, that's where you ought to be. When the snowplough comes."

She was looking at him as she spoke, expecting a nod or

a dismissive gesture of the hand to confirm that the snow-plough actually existed.

But he was not concerned with the snowplough. Instead he went on, "If I knew how people set about writing books, I'd help you. I've got knowledge. But no learning. And I used to have the strength. I remember what it was like to have strength. Now I'm like a bag of bones."

Never before had anyone offered to write with her or instead of her. She smiled at him; it was as if she was pleased at his attempt to show her such heroic kindness, as if for one brief moment she understood how he thought, but then as quickly forgot.

Later that evening she wrote the first paragraph, half a page in her writing pad. The form she had in mind, which she also made a note of, was the cadence of Gregorian chant. Simple ingenuous phrases would be developed in each chapter and through the whole into a devout recitative, and then return to the unassuming naturalness of the beginning; the two images of Christopher, the saint of legend and the putative real person, would unite and diverge like contrapuntal notes. In the elevated parts a constant striving for banal everyday reality should remain discernible; beneath the surface rhetoric the underlying depth should be ordinariness and triviality – even, if balance required it, sheer vulgarity.

And now here came the snowplough.

She had just finished writing and put down her pen when the light appeared, seeming to have its source far beneath her, pointing obliquely upwards and soon illuminating the whole night sky outside the window. Then came the roar, intensifying unremittingly and within a brief space of time filling the entire firmament, a roaring sound that incorporated a screeching and clattering and whining, an unbearable din that forced her to cover her ears with her hands. Then the vehicle itself hove into view, or at least not the actual vehicle but an enormous whirling and fuming cloud of snow, irradiated by six spotlights. The snowplough was indeed an emissary from civilisation. As it passed the noise diminished and almost died away, but then, after turning round at the end of the road, it came thundering by again.

So now the road was swept clear.

The next morning she said to Hadar, "The road is clear now."

"It really wasn't necessary," he said. "The rain would have melted the snow."

Only then did she notice the rain running down the window panes. Hadar had put on his newly washed clothes and was sitting at the table chewing a slice of bread. The fire was already burning in the stove. When she sat down opposite him she noticed that he still smelled, despite the fact that his clothes were now clean.

"When the rain stops," she said, "as soon as the rain has stopped, I'll be on my way."

"We'll see," he said.

Even through the rain pouring down the window pane the smoke from the neighbouring chimney was perfectly visible; it was being forced downwards and at times obscured the house.

"He's lit a fire today," she said.

"He's burning the paper and cardboard from the chocolate

and sugar and throat lozenges," said Hadar. "I recognise that smoke."

There was no sign of the cat. She did not ask after it, but just opened the door to see whether it was lying in the porch or sitting on the steps.

"No," said Hadar, "she's out hunting, she's not too old for that – birds and leverets and lemmings. Sometimes she's out hunting day and night for weeks at a time, is Minna."

And now the rain was stopping.

"I'll go over to your brother and say goodbye," she said. "So that he knows."

He was sitting on the sofa, his belly resting on his lap and hanging in a fold down over his knees. He had cleaned up and there were no wrapping papers lying around on the floor; his nourishing foodstuffs were piled up tidily on the kitchen worktop and on the table and chairs, and he was still panting. His bloated face was creased in a big smile: he said he had known she would come to say goodbye.

"In a couple of hours," she said. "I just want to make sure that Hadar has something to eat, at least for today."

"Does he really need food?" Olof asked. "I thought the cancer growing inside him was enough, that it filled his stomach."

He was not smiling any more as he said it. Perhaps he seriously believed that cancer was like that, not only consuming but also nourishing. He had a bag of raisins at his side, and was munching and smacking his lips continuously so that she could see that he was far from helpless.

"Is there nobody else to take care of you?" she asked. "No one except Hadar?"

He threw out his arms and raised his voice as if the question were almost incomprehensible.

"Who else would I have?" he asked. "No, Hadar is the only person I have. If we didn't have each other, well then, I don't know . . ."

When he moved his hands and arms his joints creaked as if they were completely dried out, as if nothing of all his fat had managed to penetrate and oil his skeleton.

She muttered a few words about how lucky they were to have each other despite everything, two brothers, to have their houses so wonderfully situated on the same hill and circumstances so similar in so many respects, to be forced, as it were, into mutual understanding and sympathy.

"I'd like you to take something to Hadar," said Olof. "Something of his. I can see now that it really belongs to him."

The floorboards groaned under his weight as he rose. But at least he was moving, heavily and slowly and gasping for breath. He fetched a cardboard box from the firewood bin and put it carefully in her outstretched hands. It was brown and tied up with strong twine.

"Thank you," she said.

She was thanking him on Hadar's behalf.

Before she left never to return she wanted to see the bedroom in Olof's house. She stood in the doorway, the brown carton held tight against her chest. The bedroom looked exactly as she might have expected. But there was a photograph on the pedestal table.

"Who's that?" she asked. "The woman."

She should not have enquired. It must be his mother, of course, that sad and faded and indistinct face. A bridal veil covered her hair, fastened with a rose at the front.

He had returned to the sofa after the exhausting walk with the box, and was now lying on his back.

"Minna," he said. "That's Minna. The woman I was married to. I had her photograph taken and enlarged."

"I'm so sorry," she said. "I should have realised."

The final thing she said to Olof was, "What I forgot to say about St Christopher, the Christopher I'm writing the book about, is that he protects us against sudden death. He helps those who don't want to die unprepared. I just thought I'd mention it."

She put the cardboard box on the table. "Olof sent you his greetings," she said. "He wanted you to have this, whatever it might be."

They sat and looked at the box, Hadar leaning forward slightly with his hands grasping the edge of the table, she sitting opposite him.

Finally he said, "I would never have believed it. He must be about to die. Olof. But I don't eat sweet things. If that's what it is."

The twine consisted of several strands plaited together and the knots were triple; it would be impossible to open it without some sort of implement. Hadar went on talking. He addressed himself to her and to the cardboard box, relying on her being able to understand and interpret what he was saying, his voice at times croaking and fading away.

There was indeed something unique and wonderful about brothers, he thought. Brotherhood was a natural phenomenon of the same kind as gravity or eclipses of the sun or the frost that binds the soil; it was stronger than love and hate for example. Brothers, like himself and Olof, were bound to the same umbilical cord for ever and ever. When he thought how they had slept in childhood under the same sheepskin cover and coughed the same hoarse cough from the dust out of the straw mattress, he could not help tears coming to his eyes. It was inevitable that you knew a brother down to every birthmark and wart and deformed toenail; every blemish and quality was shared so that you could even say our nose is stuffed, we're knock-kneed, our inverted navel, our big front teeth, our strong upper arms. There were no secrets between brothers; it was clearly no coincidence that people used the term blood brothers. It was significant that there were many expressions like this: brotherly hand, brotherly embrace, brotherhood, band of brothers. And brotherly love. Yes, really: brotherly love. If two men are out in the fields and one is taken and the other is left, then they are not brothers. All good nature and piety and magnanimity stem from brotherliness. It might appear at first sight that it was human beings who represented the pinnacle of creation, but in fact it was in brothers that creation achieved its perfection, in the unconditional and indissoluble bond between two brothers.

You would always do your utmost for a brother.

"I do my utmost," he said.

Being a brother involved an undertaking, a duty to embody the basic concept of brotherliness, to demonstrate it to the world or at least to your brother. Being a brother was the highest state of grace that could be bestowed on a person. To whom should you give a big cardboard box if not to your brother?

She fetched the carving knife from the kitchen worktop and

handed it to him; after all, he must actually examine the gift his brother had sent him. He cut the twine and lifted the lid.

"I knew it straight away," he said when he had seen as much as he needed to see. "I knew it was going to be that all along."

Then he got up and walked the few steps to the sofa and lay down.

It was Minna, the cat. Or Leo. The old tom. The head and the body separately. The bottom of the box was covered in congealed blood from the severed neck, and her fingers were covered in it as she picked up the stiff corpse to inspect it under the tail and between its hind legs. No, she could not find any sex, all that could be seen was the almost bare skin. This cat was neither a he nor a she. It was nothing. It had really been both Minna and Leo. Perhaps long ago it had been only the one or the other.

"It was a good thing he killed her," said Hadar. "She had to be killed anyway. It had to be done."

She looked at him. A tormented, dying man, mourning his cat. From time to time he raised his hand and stroked it in the air above his chest as if the cat were still lying there.

"So there we are," he said. "There we are."

"Well, I'll stay till tomorrow," she said. "One day here or there won't make any difference."

His hand paused in mid-air. "In that case," he said, "in that case you could take the cat out and bury it. You can bury it at the bottom of the potato patch. There's a spade inside the nearest door of the outhouse."

When she came back in after having laid the cat on the ground beneath the pine trees behind the barn, left to the crows and foxes and ravens, the head and the body separately, he said, "Now you must tell me that you've buried her, even if you've only laid her on the grass, you must tell me that you've buried her three or four feet deep."

"I've buried Minna," she said, "I buried her as deep as the spade would go."

"I think he killed her to save me the trouble," he said. "And it was neatly decapitated – we've always been clever with our hands. It wasn't so much the cardboard box he wanted to give me, it was the kill itself."

And after a while he resumed, "But he's stronger than I thought. When you kill a cat you have to be dexterous and persistent. It's a real man's job."

He lay absolutely still. He had clasped his hands across his chest; he was lying down and saving his strength in order to outlive his brother if it were at all possible. Apart from Olof's gift, the unexpected death of the cat, this could have been a completely normal day for him: painkillers, meals, dozing a bit, calls of nature, the thoughts that he kept to himself. She fetched the newspapers from the letter-box by the roadside, that day's and the previous day's, but neither of them bothered to read them. "You can light the stove with them," he said.

She went up to her bedroom and sat at the table for a while; she even wrote a short paragraph. What had to be conveyed, she noted down, was the composite nature and ambiguity of St Christopher, not who he was but what he represented. That is the only way they could be written about: not as people, only as representative figures. Fragments of oral tradition had made their way into the written sources, misunderstandings and misinterpretations and borrowings from the legends of other saints had enriched and strengthened the truth about St Christopher; actions and characteristics and perhaps even physical qualities had been attributed to him, including noxious odours that rightfully or originally belonged to Homobonus or Calixtus or Arbogast. Thus it was rumoured that he used to take up the most afflicted in his arms so that they could die in a human embrace, and that he willingly emptied the latrine barrels of the poor and the condemned in the River Morava. And that he made his abode with lepers, scraping off their uncleanness with his nails, bathing and dressing their sores, using the handle of his huge wooden spoon to feed them. She could hear Hadar talking to himself downstairs, mumbling and muttering; all she could distinguish were the curses.

When she came down his stench assailed her nostrils so strongly again that she had to hide the waves of nausea welling up inside her.

"Give yourself a break," he said. "You should rest now and then."

Once more she heated up some water on the stove and made him undress. Then she washed his entire body with rags. She rubbed the soapy water into him, and finished off by patting him dry with scraps of red and blue striped cotton flannel. And he let her do it. He lifted and twisted his arms and legs as instructed and turned on his side and stomach, and when his position allowed he talked, about himself and about her.

He really wondered whether she had fully understood how much courage and daring and fearlessness he had had to summon before he could bring himself to take her, an unknown stranger, into his house. He knew not one single thing about her other than what had been in the paper, yet he had brought her home with him. The danger an unknown person represented could almost defy belief. Being a stranger implied a degree of wildness, not to say brutality and inhumanity, never found in the local farming community; the mind of a stranger was like a bottomless pit. That was the only image he could think of: a chasm or a water-filled abyss. He was speaking now not just about strangers but about everything unknown, spirits as well as physical entities. The essential nature of existence was nothing but a constant battle against the unknown. He had to defend himself incessantly against unknown powers of every sort. In defending yourself against the unknown you revealed your true worth, your sterling qualities. When even so the unknown finally managed to invade your body, you fell ill; and when the unknown completely took over, you were dead. In your youth you could take the unknown by the horns and win, but later in life you had to rely on persistence, strategy and stamina. You could even trick the unknown into serving as an ally. You always had to think ahead, to devise plans and constantly be prepared for the worst. The most important thing was the extent to which you could depend on someone who had gone before and shown the way, someone to model yourself on.

For his part he could single out his grandfather as an example and model. His grandfather was the prototype, he the copy. Every day he devoted a few thoughts to his grandfather and the bumblebee honeypots. Most of all what happened to his grandfather at the end with regard to the bumblebee honeypots.

"What are bumblebee honeypots?" she asked.

"The bumblebees' nests in the ground," he replied. "They're bags full of honey, little bags you can squeeze honey out of, honey and nothing else."

He had an elkhound, his grandfather that is, an elkhound that stood as tall on its legs as a reindeer, with a wolf's head the way some elkhounds have, and this elkhound had learnt to seek out bumblebee nests, to recognise the scent. It would run in great circles and bark to indicate its position when it found one. And grandfather would smoke out the bees with a piece of birch-bark and squeeze the honeypot dry and collect the honey in the metal bucket he had in his rucksack. They travelled far and wide through the forests and over the bogs, did grandfather and his elkhound, in the summer when the hay-making was over. On many occasions they were away for weeks on the hunt, the hunt for bumblebee honey. Once, the time he was talking about now, they had gone westwards, far beyond Lauparlidmyran and Handskberget.

As she lifted his right arm to scrub away the grey crust of dirt in his armpit she asked, "What was it called?"

"Lauparlidmyran and Handskberget," he replied.

And behind a mound of roots by a grassy embankment, where there was no one to see it, in the grass that covered the mound, the dog had unearthed a nest. And as they leant forward over it, grandfather and the elkhound, the turf had collapsed beneath them and they had fallen down a dried-up well-shaft that had been sunk round about the beginning of time, a sixteen-foot well-shaft. And there they had sat on the gravel at the bottom; no one would look for them for the next few weeks, and no one could get themselves up out of that well, not even an elkhound. They had shared the honey between them, the bumblebee honey they had collected in the bucket, a little lick now and again. It kept them alive for as many days as it took for grandfather to wear through the back of his moleskin jacket as he sat leaning against the side of the well-shaft.

But then, when the bucket was empty, they had begun to look at one another. There was daylight from the top of the well even at night. They really scrutinised each other for the first time, and the dog saw that grandfather was actually a stranger to him and grandfather came to the conclusion that strictly speaking he did not know the dog at all. However many bumblebee nests they had tracked down together they were strangers to each other.

And it became clear to them both that before this was over, before they were somehow hauled up out of that well, one of them would have eaten the other.

"Hunger isn't the worst," she said. "It's thirst. People die when they've used up all their fluid."

Now she was busy with the other armpit.

But he pointed out that raw meat was full of liquid, that flesh was both food and drink and that the two of them down there in the well would certainly have been aware of that. If for instance you pricked holes in Olof, his brother Olof, huge amounts of fluid would seep out straight away, not rancid fat or oil as you might expect, but a liquid that actually looked like water.

So in the end it turned into a duel between his grand-father and the dog. It had become a question of persistence, wakefulness and patience, and when they were eventually discovered – by a man who chanced upon the hole in the ground while out looking for his horses – it was quite obvious that one of them had undoubtedly eaten the other.

She did not ask who had eaten whom. He would never have told her the story if it had been the elkhound that had eaten his grandfather.

She fetched her toothbrush and toothpaste and brushed his teeth. They really were amazingly well preserved. He opened his mouth wide for her, and as she held his lips with her thumb and forefinger, brushing and rubbing until his gums began to bleed, she said, "I wonder what it tastes like, bumblebee honey."

Then, when she could make him no cleaner, before she gave him back his clothes, she bent down and smelt him, from the top of his head to the soles of his feet, and she found that the stench was just as bad as ever. It came from the pores of his skin and from his mouth and nostrils and suppurating eyes and from his ears and his navel. She had also intended trimming his nails and hair, the little fringe round his skull, but now she decided against it. His skin had taken on an almost metallic shine, matt yellow with bluish-white glints in the changing light.

"Of course," he said, "of course, I could have just left you to carry on with your own life."

Later in the afternoon, when he had taken his painkillers, he said, "When I inherit from Olof, I'm going to demolish his house, and out of the timber I'm going to build a sauna, a real Finnish sauna with a cobblestone hearth.

"That's one subject," he said, "that I'm sure you know nothing about."

No amount of washing, scrubbing and scraping could in

any way compare to sweating. Brushes and water merely touched the surface, whereas sweat emerged from within, and it was from within that uncleanness arose. It was what came out of a person that made him unclean.

He had been thinking about it for some time: a sauna, if only Olof would have the decency to die soon. He certainly did not want to deny a dying man the right to struggle for life, to prolong his own suffering, but Olof was taking things rather too far in that respect. But, when the day came, he would sit in the sauna that he had built with the wood dismantled from Olof's house and sweat out all the uncleanness and all the odours – that was the only natural and fitting way for a man, a man was made to sweat, and as long as a man was doing heavy work and sweating he never needed to wash. If the sweat of his own life had been collected in a hollow in the ground, it would have made a sizeable lake – no, not a lake, a marsh, a muddy tarn, a bottomless quagmire. Because men's sweat, he would have her know, was not thin and watery; no – it was like gruel or limewash, it was strong and rich in ingredients; it did not run freely and easily but had to be squeezed out through the pores like mushy peas through a strainer.

Of course it was only right and proper that women should sweat too, but women's sweat did not have the profound significance of men's sweat. In the past there had been a woman who had sweated with him, so to speak, and his sweat had been diluted by hers, and that was how he knew that women's sweat was thin and translucent; it flowed easily, frivolously even, out of women's smooth skin, and it had hardly any smell at all. If you got it up your nose it reminded you of birch sap. Women were indifferent to sweat, it was unrelated to dirtiness or cleanliness, for them it represented nothing and meant nothing.

So he would sit on his own over there in the sauna that he would build with Olof's inheritance; she wouldn't need to be there to help him – he would support his head in his hands and force out so much sweat that no uncleanness and nothing superfluous or alien and no sickness would remain in him.

Before evening came she went over to see Olof. "Go on!" said Hadar. "You go! After all, it's not your concern if I die here alone!"

Olof had fallen asleep at the table, a half-eaten bar of chocolate sticking out of the corner of his mouth, his head and arms resting on the table-top.

She woke him by saying, "I won't be leaving until tomorrow."

He sat up and pushed the chocolate into his mouth. "I was sitting thinking," he said as he chewed. "I was thinking of you travelling to the ends of the earth by bus and train and aeroplane."

He was sweating profusely, as if his house were already a sauna.

She sat down. Then she asked, "Why do you hate him? Why do you hate Hadar?"

At this he raised his arms from the table and held out both palms towards her. "I don't!" he said, "I don't hate Hadar! He's my brother!"

And he assured her, "The man who hates his brother is in eternal darkness, he who hates his brother is a murderer."

No, as a brother-hater he was hardly even mediocre!

His sugar-sodden brain had been stimulated by her question.

"But you wish him dead," she said.

"Dead?" he responded. "I can't say I remember that. Dead?"

So she reminded him about the cat. The cat in the cardboard box.

"Oh, that was nothing," said Olof. "I'd already forgotten that."

She must understand that Hadar had been a fine, splendid, energetic fellow before the cancer had begun to eat into him, a first-born brother whom you could respect, even try to emulate!

All through his childhood and youth he had put a lot of time and effort into his attempts to be a second Hadar. It had been such a thrill for him when he was passed an article of clothing or a pair of shoes that Hadar had grown out of, or a sheath knife that had become too blunt for him. And when he was allowed to lie under Hadar's sheepskin he had been filled with such jubilant happiness and blissful devotion that he could not get to sleep for the life of him.

It was a wretched shame that they had had to grow up. If they had been able to remain children, or at least young men, they would still have been able to offer one another consolation and encouragement today, they would still be lying at their mother's side, as it were, one at each breast, being suckled with sweet milk.

It was adulthood that had separated them.

For himself adulthood had brought sorrow and melancholy. Hadar had been afflicted by it as if by a sickness of the soul: he had become a thief and a swindler and evildoer.

It brought tears to his eyes now when he thought of everything he had learnt from Hadar: swearing, carving willow pipes and pulling the legs off little frogs, all the secrets of the human body, snaring pike, the song about the girl sitting on the roof, fermenting birch sap, whistling between his front teeth. Yes, he had learnt everything from Hadar; without Hadar's knowledge he would not have known how life should be lived.

"You ought to go over to him," she said. "I can support you for that short distance."

But it was completely out of the question, he could only guffaw at such a foolish notion – to the extent that he was still able to guffaw nowadays, since people with a heart condition had to avoid such exertion. No, Hadar would rip the clothes off his body straight away or at least grab for himself what little he happened to have in his pockets, or he would rob him of his emotional equilibrium and perhaps even his reason with his lies and his curses, or – and this was the most likely – he would stab him with his knife. That was how he had been ever since they were grown up and the farm had been divided between them.

He, Hadar, had poached the milk from his, Olof's, cows. He had pilfered the birch wood and peat from his land, he had stolen his socks and flannel shirts from the washing line, he had lifted the shingles from his roof so that the sugar and sugar lumps in his attic would dissolve in the rain, he had commandeered the memory of their grandfather and maintained that it was he, Hadar, who was so perfectly like him, and that he, Olof, displayed not a single trait of him; and he had filched his electricity supply through illegal connections. It was impossible to recall everything he had done. He was not as unforgiving as Hadar, so he allowed himself to forget this and that. Like the fact that Hadar blasted Minna's lilac bush to pieces with a shotgun, just when it was in bloom. And that he cut Minna with his knife.

"Minna?" she said. "Minna, your wife?"

But he had to add that he felt some sympathy with Hadar, even a share of his guilt. No one could say that he simply wished him dead; he was not as malevolent and unloving as that. Now that Hadar was lying there so burnt out and haggard and abandoned by everyone. But he did not begrudge him his pain, nor his liberation from pain, the one first and the other second, nor did he begrudge him his shrinking and shrivelling like a dried squirrel-pelt. No, he did not wish death upon Hadar, but he was willing to admit that he, as his brother, might soon have a right to expect it for him. Ah yes, a calm and satisfying death at the end. That's how he felt. Then, with Hadar finally gone, then he himself, for his own part, having mourned for a suitable period, would emerge from his cocoon like one of those colourful variegated summer butterflies and start enjoying life to the full at last.

He used exactly those words: to the full. He had laid his heavy, swollen, blue-veined hands on the table in front of him.

It had started snowing again, papery flakes that seemed to hang motionless in the air.

That evening too she sat at her writing table for a couple of hours.

She was repeating herself frequently, but she seemed not to be troubled by it. And her few readers would probably not even notice, they might actually need a certain amount of repetition; repetition helped them to recognise themselves, and it was thanks to repetition that the written word became deceptively similar to the rest of existence. And after all it was not the actual words that mattered, but what was being demonstrated or exemplified.

Late one evening St Christopher stopped at the Gooseblood Inn at Ula. The landlord served him apple brandy with honey. Sweating profusely, Christopher drank, holding the goblet between his palms because of the calluses on his fingers. And the innkeeper wanted to know what business he was travelling on and who he was and what sort of life he led.

"Really and truly," said Christopher, "I don't lead a life in the usual sense of the expression. My duty is to pursue a certain course as an experiment. I am part representative, part representation. Just like a figure in a chronicle or a mystery play."

"It seems to me," said the innkeeper, "to be a severe case of artifice."

"Not at all," said Christopher. "For me there is no other way of life but that of imitation. Which at the same time means being an exemplar."

"For me," said the innkeeper, "it would be the most horrendous torment never to be myself, not to be able to arrange my existence in accordance with my own nature." As he spoke he picked at his teeth with a chicken claw, belching intermittently.

"The difference between being and appearing to be is not as significant as people generally believe," said Christopher. "In my case the distinction is blurred. I am what I represent. I bear my representative role exactly as I bear everything else.

Representation is purely and simply a matter of bearing. We are only ourselves when we represent someone or something we really believe in."

"Is that a duty?" the innkeeper asked.

"Yes," said St Christopher. "It is a duty."

Her writing was getting bigger and more angular than usual. It was probably because of the unaccustomed light and the weariness of her hand after the activities of the day.

On the morning of the third day she shovelled away the snow that had fallen in the night. She burnt the fur hat that had been lying outside the kitchen door. "If you get another cat," she said, "you'll have to look out a new hat for it."

No, he would never again let himself be tied to anyone, not a single living being.

She saw the snowplough drive past, but showed no sign of agitation. Having fetched the newspaper from the box at the roadside she sat down at the table to read it. When Hadar saw what she was doing, he said, "No, we shouldn't read the paper, we should steer clear of disaster and distress. We should live as quiet a life as lichen. We can use the paper to light the stove."

So she screwed up the paper and stuffed it into the stove.

It was obviously easiest for him to control his pain if he lay on his back; he stared up at the ceiling as he continued talking about the art of living like lichen.

People did not understand slowness, they only understood things that moved at their own pace. They did not understand the mountain eroding or the pine forest dying or the stones pushing up through the soil; they did not understand their own nails and how they grew. They could accept time, but not slowness. That was why people read newspapers, to fill themselves up with events and time. But slowness was so much stronger and more tenacious than time; time soon came to an end, but slowness almost never ended. Slowness contained pretty well everything simultaneously. Whereas time itself was like mosquitoes and gnats, slowness was like a large ruminant lying down and chewing the cud. People who gave themselves up to time had no real past, only one that was wasted, consumed and extinguished. And without a past, man was merely a puff of wind. A conscientiously and slowly lived past – that was the only raw material a steadfast human being could be made of.

Presumably this was his way of asking about her past.

"I've burnt the paper," she said. "I put it in the stove."

He raised his arm and stretched out a hand as if to touch her.

"Ah, everybody has it in them to become one of us ordinary folk," he said.

More often than not he lay with his arms folded across his stomach, as if trying to embrace his pain. He was mostly silent, sometimes muttering or coughing out a word or two, never sounding as if he expected an answer. There were no answers. He might say: "The flies live in the cow dung to survive the winter." Or: "You could help me kill Olof." Or: "I can feel her teeth gnawing at a new part of my gut."

"Whose?" she asked.

"The cancer's."

Or: "Do you think Olof's got enough wood to last?"

On one of the first few days, perhaps the third, but it might equally well have been the seventh or the tenth, he said, "The doll I used to have, I suppose it's rotted away."

"What doll?" she said.

"The wooden doll. The doll that was carved out of a piece of birch. The doll that was painted in yellow ochre and light blue and zinc white, the one that had a red ribbon under her chin. She looked as real as a human hand or finger. The doll that I had when I was little."

"When you were little?" she said. "When you were a child?"

Yes, he had had a childhood. It might sound improbable, but it was true – a long time ago, but a childhood nevertheless.

To a large extent he had shared it with Olof. They had both been slender-limbed and had childish thoughts and hunted squirrels with wooden arrows.

And through all that childhood, from the beginning to the end as far as he could remember, that wooden doll had been his. His grandfather had carved her. She had lain under his shirt when he was in the forest and down by the lake, she had listened when he whistled and talked, she had slept in his bed at night, she had been closer to him than any other living being. And after Olof got his teeth and learnt to walk, a horse had been carved for him, so that he would not steal the doll and turn her into a formless lump.

Yes, when he thought of his childhood it was the doll that came to mind, how beautiful she was and smooth to the touch and faithful to him and desirable to Olof and warm to hug under the eiderdown or sheepskin.

"A wooden doll?"

"Yes, a wooden doll."

But the day his grandfather was found, his grandfather and the gnawed dog bones – the marks of teeth had been clearly visible on the skull and the ribs – that was the day he had decided that his childhood was over as far as he was concerned. In the end the childishness of childhood had aroused his disgust, and he had crept under the cow shed, right in past the timber from the old sheep byre that had stood where Olof's house would later be built, and there he had laid the doll on a flat stone and stroked her belly for the last time.

If someone could crawl under it now, he said, if anybody were brave enough to get under the cow shed and look carefully, then it might be possible to find the doll again, the doll that had lain there all his life, assuming that Olof had not found her long before and desecrated her and burnt her up on the wood stove. The thought had occurred to him time and time again, ever since this troublesome illness had set upon him and started gnawing at him: if only he had had his doll.

Crawling on her hands and knees she finally found the flat rock, having scraped her fingertips raw on splinters and stones as she felt ahead of her, and on it there was indeed a piece of wood, covered in dust and cobwebs. She tucked it under her coat and carried it out into the light.

Yes, it could have been a doll, it might really have been a doll before the paint flaked off and nearly all the uneven shape had worn away; there might have been a head and arms and shoulders and feet.

Hadar was sitting upright on the sofa. He seized the piece of wood straight away with both hands and held it up in front of him. His jaw dropped so that the wrinkles in his face almost disappeared, and saliva was trickling from the corner of his mouth. When at last he tried to say something, he sounded almost too breathless to speak.

Yes, that really was her, that was his doll. Olof had not discovered her and she had not rotted away. He had chosen the one and only perfect flat stone for her; even at that age his cunning had been far greater than Olof's. It was incredible, indeed it was a miracle that she had been preserved for him in this way, so untouched and virginal; it was as if she had risen from the dead. There must be some hidden meaning behind it. "Can you see," he said, "the way she's sort of smiling with her eyes and how fresh the colour is in her face and how well carved her knees and feet are?"

"Yes," she said, "it's remarkable."

"Can I keep her with me at night?" he asked.

"You don't have to ask me," she said.

"Who else should I ask?" he said.

She told Olof later on. "Hadar has got his doll back," she said, "the wooden doll he had when he was a child."

"That's not possible," said Olof. "He said he'd tied her to a stone and thrown her into the lake."

Olof had started coughing. That was probably how he would die, in the middle of a fit of coughing.

"It was under the cow shed," she said, "on a flat rock."

"The bastard," he said. "I hunted and hunted for her! How I hunted!"

But then Olof wanted to talk about something else, he seemed to need to. "So you're writing?" he said. "You're writing that book. You've not only got Hadar, but the book as well."

She would soon be on her way, she reminded him, but she

could stay for a little while longer. Even though she was staying, she was really on her way at the same time, if he saw what she meant. Yes, she was writing and she had Hadar, but neither of them was really any trouble to her. She wrote a bit every evening, whereas before she used to write in the mornings. Writing in the evenings felt quite natural to her now. You just decided on a subject for yourself. There was scope for anything on any subject. She felt more or less at home up here, and even, she said, a sort of involvement that was hard to explain in his, Olof's, and his brother's, Hadar's, joint undertaking, this futile competition to extend their lives, which she could not help but regard as artistic, representing something beyond itself, and in some respects similar to her own endeavours. Yes, she was happy here. The deadly but at the same time absurd seriousness of their situation, the mixture of devotion to the task and resigned indifference, that was just the kind of thing that filled her with a sense of temporary belonging. She had always tried to avoid over-estimating the worth of her own life and thus exploiting it too inconsiderately. She was not an important writer, and had never wanted to be; she just wrote.

He looked at her steadily, the fat beneath the skin of his face seeming to stiffen in his vain effort to try to interpret and understand what she was saying. "I could read one of the books you've written," he said.

But that was not something she was keen to encourage. No, it would be best not to expend his mental energies on reading or other pointless activities; Hadar presumably never would. And he was not by nature one of her readers: people who read her books did not do so purposefully and conscientiously as he would; her readers actually knew nothing of what they were entering into, nor did they basically know anything of life. They lived in towns in the south and reading was no more than one of their idle pursuits. Quite honestly she knew nothing about them, she did not understand them. They just happened to pick up one of her books, in exactly the same way that she just chanced upon some subject or other.

That day he was eating macaroons and dark red jam from a square-sided jar. "But how did we get on to this?" she asked.

"We were talking about the doll," Olof reminded her. "That doll of Hadar's."

"Olof is fine," she said to Hadar. "He's getting stronger every day. He could live for many more years yet."

"One day you say he ought to be looked after," said Hadar, "and the next you maintain that he's hale and hearty."

When he wanted to get up off the sofa now he always expected her to support him; he put out the palms of his hands towards her as if he were defending himself and trying to push her away at the same time as he was appealing for help.

"The heart is like that," he said. "Even if it seems all right it can soon start racing and then just collapse. The heart is like some infernal machine."

She had put the bucket at the foot of the sofa. As he sat on it he said, "With cancer everything is neat and tidy. She grinds away and does what she has to and you know where you are with her. It's not simply a matter of chance that I'm the one who's got cancer and he that's got the weak heart. Olof has always been unreliable and treacherous: it was obvious that he would be the one to have the heart condition."

Something had happened to his smell: she was no longer aware of it. When she came down in the mornings she was vaguely and fleetingly reminded of it, but it had stopped impinging on her, it was just a memory.

When he was lying on the sofa again, he said, "And miracles do happen, we know that, miracles do happen. People rise from the dead and reptiles can grow wings and start to fly. Cancer can melt away like a lump of ice that's dropped inside your shirt."

"Do you really think so?" she asked.

"That's the only thing you can be sure of," he said. "That anything is possible. Miracles can happen, that's the one thing that is certain."

Even the smell from the bucket did not seem unpleasant to her as she carried it out and emptied it in the snow below the house.

But when she told him, when she said that at first she had found his smell obnoxious, even using the word stench, and that that was why she had washed his clothes and his body so thoroughly, but that now his peculiar odour had died away or been eradicated, he said, "I smell the same as I did before. I smell more acrid every day. It's a terrible torment for me. But I was too tactful to mention it."

From Hadar's window she kept an eye on Olof's chimney and its smoke signals. When it turned colder the smoke became thinner and lighter and rose upwards continuously; on the few days when it started to thaw it was darker and more irregular, occasionally disappearing altogether. She devoted nearly all her free time to this poignant and meaningful smoke. She watched it while conversing with Hadar or listening to his groans or snores. She kept the path between the houses open, so that if necessary she could run down there in less than a minute.

Sometimes Hadar would say, "It wasn't for his sake that you were brought here!"

When he was asleep, in the periods when his painkillers had sent him to sleep, she would go and sit with Olof. It was unbelievable that it was only a few days before, or a couple of weeks or a month, that Hadar had driven his car into the village and brought her back, and that he had had the strength to listen to her lecture without slipping from consciousness or complaining.

She could not help saying to Olof one day, "It's granted to very few people to have something to live for right up to the very end and be able to enjoy life the way you do, like the way you're enjoying those liquorice bootlaces."

"This isn't enjoyment," he said. "I'm feeding myself."

No, he was certainly not indulging in something as superficial and shameful as enjoyment, he had never done that. There was no room in his life for such stuff and nonsense as physical pleasures, not to mention spiritual. No, he lived purely and simply for Hadar's sake, or, more precisely, for his own sake but in relation to Hadar. He would be extremely annoyed if he discovered a pleasure or a comfort or anything else that would provide a further reason for living. He would not want anything on the lines of Hadar's wooden doll. A pleasure could at most lead to something as ridiculous and transitory as satisfaction. He was delighted that his life was as simple as it was, that it had but one sole purpose. That simplicity suited him. It was dangerous to divide life up between too many goals: everything beyond the one, the one and only, objective would be meaningless, which indeed it was.

As far as he was concerned he could do no better than to refer her to the trees, the fir trees, but in particular the pines, and the way they lived their lives and held their own.

He could not manage to sit upright even when he was talking. The struggle to breathe just made him bloat and ferment even more, and his cheeks and the folds of flesh under his chin trembled and shook.

Trees, he pointed out to her, had one single function in life: they had to stand upright. Beyond that they were nothing special. The individual tree was exclusively concerned with standing upright; both the roots and the crown were inspired in every fibre by this one purpose, not to let the whole tree fall down. He would like to regard himself as a tree, a tall pine tree up here on the mountainside.

"I see," she said, "I understand. I see what you mean."

He was silent for a moment before concluding his exposition, sinking down and swelling out even more at the sides.

If she thought he was a hedonist, then she was greatly mistaken. He would go so far as to say that on the whole there were no hedonists up here; hedonists were necessarily kept away by the cold and the meagreness of the soil. In southern Sweden there were hedonists, even voluptuaries, but not here. That did not mean, however, that he was completely ignorant on the subject of pleasure, that he did not know what pleasure was; no, she was not to think that.

So she asked him to tell her what he knew about pleasure.

It had been in his early childhood, it was a memory that had followed him throughout his life, not just followed him but guided him, perhaps even dominated him.

He had had a grandfather who collected bumblebee honey. He used to go out looking for bumblebee nests with his dog, and he would put the honey in a jar in his rucksack. In the end he went missing in the forest, and his remains were discovered only long afterwards in a well on a deserted property and hauled up by bucket. But he had left a glass jar in the pantry, a small glass jar of bumblebee honey, behind the casks of herring and jars of bilberries and bottles of lingonberry juice, a glass jar with a wooden lid – and nobody could recall anything about it. He, Olof, who was still a small child and could creep in anywhere and remain unseen, he squeezed in under the bottom shelf in the pantry and found this glass jar. And he prized off the lid and dug out the bumblebee honey with his fingers, licking it off them and eating it.

That was how he came to taste pure sweetness for the first time in his life, a sweetness that was not mixed with anything else but was simply itself, the sweetest taste a human being can experience. The honey permeated his whole being and transported him into a state of utter bliss and rapture. It was a moment of perfect pleasure, a state he had striven to recreate for himself unceasingly all the rest of his life, though by and large in vain. When he had licked the glass jar so clean that it looked as if it had been washed out with spring water, and when he had pushed aside the herring casks and the pots and bottles and crawled out on to the floor again, he was no longer the same person.

"But pleasure," he said, "no, pleasure is still not the right word for it. How do you express the inexpressible? If I knew the right word I would say it."

"Hadar must be awake by now," she said. "He shouts for me when he wakes up."

"Has he started using his knife on you yet?" asked Olof.

"Hadar isn't like that," she said. "Mostly he sleeps. And he doesn't stink any more. The stench was really the only thing about Hadar that was hard to bear."

"Where are you?" Hadar was shouting. "Where are you?"

"I'm here," she said.

He was sitting on the sofa with his back to the window, trying to rub some life into his numb and yellowing face with the arthritic fingers of his right hand.

"It makes me uneasy when you're not here," he said. "You never know."

"I go where I want," she said. "I can go off whenever I feel like it."

"I hope you're not going over to Olof," he said. "You never know what he might get up to. I've been afraid of him all my life."

She sat down at the table. "Olof says you stabbed his wife, his Minna, with your knife," she said. She pretended to be looking out at the snowdrifts.

"His Minna?" said Hadar. "Olof's Minna? Is that what he says?"

"Minna was his wife," she said. "And he says you stabbed her."

Hadar clenched his fist and let it drop on to his thigh. "She wasn't his," he said. "Olof has never known what it means to own anything, he's just taken for himself, never been able to own anything. Ownership is a man's job."

"Why should Olof tell lies?" she asked. "With his heart

65

condition and his shortness of breath, why should he lie?"

"We are the way we are," said Hadar, "the way we're made, the way we've made one another. Olof says first one thing and then another, he does nothing but talk. What little strength he has is confined to his mouth. I never speak, I keep my mouth shut, and may God bless me for it."

No, he didn't want to say anything about Minna, Olof's wife. "I'm hungry," he said. "Why can't I have bacon and barley porridge and swedes any more?"

He was nearly always hungry. But he vomited up most of the food she made for him. The only things he could keep down now were porridge and gruel.

He remembered a conversation they had once had in their youth, he and Olof, in the times when they had still been on speaking terms. He could remember it word for word. It was after their mother had died and they had buried her.

"She was a good person," one of them had said. And the other had replied, "No, she wasn't!"

"She stroked our heads and kissed us and she never hit us. And she dressed us in the mornings so that we wouldn't freeze to death. She wanted us to be happy. She poured syrup on our porridge for us."

"People have always done that, poured something on barley gruel for children. Otherwise you have to give it to the pigs."

"And she gave us life."

"She had to, she couldn't go around pregnant for ever."

"And she played the zither to us and sang, and she helped us with our sums in our arithmetic books. And she sewed us a football out of grandfather's leather bag. That was pure goodness!"

"A human being can't be good. Goodness is made up of an infinite number of parts. No one can possess them all."

"Which of you said that?" she asked.

"It could have been me," said Hadar. "Yes, it must have been me."

He was sorry that he could not immediately say which of them had said one thing and which the other. Any amount of confusion was possible between brothers. But now he remembered that it was Olof who had gone on to say, "You've never approved of goodness! You just find goodness laughable. You've always mocked goodness. And now you're even unwilling to admit that your mother was good!"

And Olof had spat at Hadar when he said this.

"She was like everyone else," Hadar had said. "There was nothing special about her."

At that Olof had punched him in the stomach with his fist, right where the cancer had subsequently taken root, and shouted at him, "You should honour your mother, or you'll come to a sorry end! Goodness isn't a mixture of this and that, goodness is good in itself and good in its effects! If you say anything different I'll hit you with these handlebars until you learn!"

He really did have a pair of bicycle handlebars in his hand and was brandishing them violently. Hadar had taken a few steps back and said, "Nothing is pure and unmixed, everything is cloudy and contaminated. If pure goodness existed it would be impossible to see it, it would be as invisible as the air!"

Then Olof had pitched into him with the handlebars, chrome-plated handlebars with the bell still attached.

"Our mother was good!" he had screamed. "It's from her

we get our own goodness! Mother was pure and untainted! And goodness will always triumph! If we didn't have goodness, we'd be bereft and inadequate. Don't you ever forget that, for as long as you live!"

And he had beaten Hadar about the arms and legs and ankles, even across the back of his head and his kneecaps and ribs and throat, and the bell had rung throughout.

So ended Hadar's story of the conversation he remembered word for word.

"Well?" she said. "What happened next?"

No, he couldn't remember any more, there was no next. That was how memory was: it always started abruptly and ended abruptly; it was like the cry of a capercaillie or the time signal on the wireless; all memories were chopped off at both ends.

And this was a particular memory that he called to mind from time to time so that he could always be sure of remembering it.

"For Olof's sake," he said. "It was Olof's express wish, after all."

That night she was woken by something pressing on the top of her head and forehead. She was lying on her back with her hands clasped over her chest. Further down the bedcover lay the book she had been reading before she fell asleep: The Golden Legend.

It was Hadar; he was holding his hand on her head, trying to look at her despite the darkness.

"You're asleep," he said. "Yes, you certainly can sleep."

"How did you get up here?" she asked.

"I walked," he said. "I just climbed the stairs."

"You'll kill yourself going down again," she said. "You'll end up as a pile of bones in the hall."

"I've got to tell you the facts about Minna," he said. "You ought to know how it was. How it was with Minna and me and why I had to give her a little nick with my knife."

She always woke up very slowly, in fact she often lay absolutely still with her eyes open for half an hour after waking. He was feeling her forehead and temples as if trying to check whether her temperature was raised. She gently lifted his hand away.

"Minna?" she said. "What Minna?"

"Olof's woman," he said. "The woman who married Olof."

Hadn't Olof said anything about Minna, hadn't he shown her the photograph and hadn't he talked about the meals she used to make?

"No. He hasn't said anything."

Well, that was how it had been: she had really come with Olof, she had followed him of her own free will from Risliden where he had found her, and she had agreed to marry him. She had been young and Olof had been young and he, Hadar, had been young too. She hadn't been exactly pretty – no, she was no beauty – but she was healthy and shapely, and when he came to think of her on a night like this, then all in all she was an attractive and desirable creature. She had a permanent smell of soap.

She was fair – no, not just fair-skinned but pale, or more accurately, white. Her hair was white and her eyebrows were white and so were her eyelashes. What little colour she had was in her eyes and lips and around her fingernails and in the blood that was visible under her skin.

"There's a name for that," he said.

"Yes," she said, "it has a name."

She was so white that if it had been her he was sitting with on the edge of the bed like this she would have appeared nearly as light as by day. That was what Minna was like.

He had never involved himself. It had nothing to do with him. Olof had got himself a woman, that was all there was to it. Olof had needed a woman, so he had gone off, even as far as Risliden, and had apparently found a suitable one.

Well, it so happened that she came over to him, Hadar, for a taste of bacon. She was never allowed to make anything but cakes and bilberry gruel and semolina pudding and fruit-syrup and pancakes with vanilla-flavoured sugar. She had been nearly breaking into sobs as she spoke. She would slip over when Olof was in the forest or down on the lake and would sit on the chair nearest the door and talk; her voice was like her hair and eyebrows, it was pale and insubstantial, not to say pitiful, yet at the same time beautiful. It sounded like a bird.

She had said how lonely it was in this village that consisted of only two little cottages and their outhouses, and that she was homesick for Risliden. Or rather not Risliden but the bacon in Risliden.

It had to be cut thick and the rind should be left on and it should be fried slowly so that the fat stayed light and succulent and could be mixed with the mashed potato. If she had known that she would have to do without salty food, that there would never be any salt again in her life, then Olof would never have been able to fool her and seduce her. At home in Risliden she had never imagined there could be a life without bacon of one kind or another. But it had never occurred to her to ask Olof about a thing like that, and now it was all too late.

Hadar propped himself against the bed and leant over her to make sure she could hear everything he said. She interrupted him to ask, "Was she backward? Was Minna feeble-minded?"

Oh no, she was a thinking person to an exceptional degree; she could think better and more fully than any other person he had ever met. Even her thoughts on bacon showed that.

And she could describe sweet food, even the sensation and experience of sweetness: the first bites were as they should be, neither better nor worse than others; they were like gifts from God of any kind. But after another mouthful or two a glorious fullness would rapidly come upon you, you would think you had had just as much as you needed, you would feel the sweetness going to your head almost like some kind of intoxication. And then on the tenth or fifteenth mouthful you would be sated, it would suddenly become impossible to force down another spoonful or morsel or crumb, and finally this repletion would turn into misgivings, discomfort and nausea.

That was how powerful sweetness was, but it could not satisfy your hunger in the long term.

That was what Minna used to say.

"And if you can say that, you're not feeble-minded."

When they had eaten the bacon and the potatoes, having stood side by side at the stove boiling the potatoes and frying the bacon, he had lain with her, or rather, they had lain with each other, he Hadar and she Minna.

Olof had still been in his boat out on the lake, or in the forest with his axe and saw. Whatever Olof did he needed more time than seemed reasonable. Even then his sugar fat had begun to expand and weigh him down.

They had lain with each other on a padded quilt that he had spread out on the floor between the table and the sofa. They had spread the quilt out together.

She interrupted him again.

"But why," she asked, "why did you have to cut her with your knife?"

"I didn't cut her," said Hadar. "I just nicked her."

And he waved his arm in front of her face to show her the difference between cutting and nicking.

After a while she had come back again. Who can live without salt pork, or for that matter new potatoes that you dip in coarse salt, or salt herring that have been soaked in water for an hour? And everything had happened all over again: they had stood next to each other in the heat of the stove, they had eaten, they had spread out the padded quilt. They had enjoyed together the energy and the happiness that the salty food gave them.

And he had realised that it would all repeat itself – everything constantly begins again from the beginning, the rivers empty into the sea unceasingly and yet the sea never fills up – she would come back to him so that they could spread the padded quilt, and Olof would sit in his boat on the lake or be out in the forest, and every time they would do exactly the same.

He had feared that his memory would get muddled and confused. There was nothing he was more worried about than his memory clouding over. So in order not to lose count he had carefully made two nicks on the inside of her thighs.

That was what hunters did too, any hunter would: they

would never forget the first time they killed an animal, but as soon as the second time came they would cut two notches in the butt of their gun, one for the unforgettable occasion and one for the next, and they would continue thus until they were too feeble and weak-sighted to hunt any more.

It was so easy. And painless. There was no sharper sheath knife than his, it would slice through bacon under its own weight, and he could have taken out tonsils and appendixes with it.

The tiny little marks on her skin gradually, or rather very quickly, healed up – Minna had fast-healing flesh that is only found in strong and healthy families – and when he next lay with her, when they lay with each other again, he was able to count the scars with his fingertips. He also clearly remembered that she had often, in fact always, guided his hand to the scars, the fingertips of his right hand; she too had been afraid he would lose count.

That's what those marks on the skin on the inside of her thighs had been. Yes, that's what his and her scratches were about, the little wounds that one of them had cut in the other, he and Minna.

He wanted her to know.

He was so tired now that he actually rested his cheek on her pillow. She sat up and carefully lifted him off.

"You must go back to sleep," she said. "You can talk to me as much as you like during the day, I'll listen, you can tell me whatever you wish, we have all the time in the world."

"It's at night I need to talk," said Hadar.

"I'll help you down the stairs," she said. "I'll support you.

Tomorrow you can talk about anything you want to, whatever comes into your head."

But when morning came he was silent. He lay with his eyes closed so that she would not be tempted to speak to him; even when she fed him with gruel and croutons he kept his eyes closed.

No, they never wanted to tell her about their lives, Hadar and Olof, nor did she ever demand that they did so.

But from time to time she would note down something or other in the margin of her writing pad that must have meant a lot to them. When they were alive, so to speak.

Cows, she wrote. Sheep and pigs. Horses. Logs. Weather.

On one occasion she wrote: Olof will die soon.

A few pages further on she noted: Hadar is dying now.

And almost as if Hadar had seen the little marginal note and wanted to expand on it and clarify it, he said a few words one evening about the special nature of his situation. Even dying was a way of life, he assured her; it was life of the very highest order, an enhanced form of existence in which nothing could really be expressed in words or exemplified any more; you simply were, there was nothing more than that, you just made the greatest effort you could to hold on to life so that it would not remain eternally unfinished. If a dying man spoke, it was not to express anything in particular, it was only to pass the time.

His father had lain up in her little bedroom and talked. Sometimes he, Hadar, had sat there for a while and listened. On the whole it had been meaningless. Nothing had been said that he hadn't heard thousands of times before. His father's last words were about the gatepost up by the milk-churn stand needing to be moved two feet to the right. The gateway was far too narrow when you hauled in the timber, especially when it was the tall and crooked birch trees from up on Handskberget.

Her story of St Christopher was becoming more and more free; she lacked source material. She devoted a whole chapter to his dog-like head, to the incongruous idea that his head resembled that of a schnauzer, and that he howled like a dog when he was spoken to and tore at the throats or legs of lone travellers if he was provoked. This elaboration of the legend originated from German sources in the tenth century; it simply illustrated the difference between the oriental and the German way of thinking. She used words like profanation and brutalisation. Hagiography is the freest of all the arts, she wrote. He may perhaps have borne a remote resemblance to a St Bernard, but she would venture no further than that.

And she invented a bishop who taught St Christopher and became his companion. He cooked soup for him and washed his clothes and wrote a description of all the miracles that occurred around him. He was later to act as a witness in the canonisation process. Hadar and Olof had stopped asking her about the book she was writing; they were no longer inquisitive – they had understood everything about the book, and they were too weary.

She wrote a letter to her publisher. When the opportunity presented itself she would post it.

"I have stayed on here for a few days," she wrote, "in a small village called Övreberg. I am renting an attic room with a mansard roof. You must not be disappointed if my book is not ready by the spring. Disappointed is the wrong word, of course – my books are hardly an asset to your list.

But you know what I mean. I cannot seem to write as simply and factually as I had intended. You won't be able to publish it in your little series of miscellaneous biographies. You don't need to send me any money; I can manage.

"My landlord is an elderly gentleman with a rich and varied experience of life. He is rather ailing. I am greatly enjoying his stories. It is quite cold up here, colder than I had expected. I wish I had brought woollen underclothes with me. I'll let you know when I have a more or less fixed address."

One day she tried talking to Olof about the wife he had had.

"He didn't stab her with his knife," she said. "Hadar didn't stab Minna, he just used the knife to make scratches."

Olof too now lay day and night unmoving on his sofa. He did not sit up when she opened the door and came in; he did not even bother to turn his head. She put in front of him what he needed each day, packets of food on the chair at the head of the sofa, the enamel pail at the foot.

This time however he tried to heave himself up, and managed to get his lower arm and elbow under his midriff and turn his torso towards her.

"Did Hadar say that?" he asked. "Is that what Hadar says?"

"Yes," she said. "He scratched so carefully that she hardly felt it."

It was difficult for Olof to breathe when he was not lying flat on his back. His voice wheezed, and sometimes cracked. "He cut her," he said, "he cut the way you do when you open bags of fertiliser. If I had flesh and blood right under my skin like other people I'd take my knife and cut so that you could see. Blood and raw flesh. He cut exactly the way I would cut."

"He says she went along with it," she said. "She didn't mind, he says."

"Hadar never understood how passive and pious she was," said Olof. "She was mine, that was why he tortured her. It was me he should have cut, but he wasn't man enough to do that."

"What did you do about it?" she asked. "What did you do for Minna?"

"What could I do?" he asked. "What can you do when you're up against a person like Hadar?"

The pail was half full; she would have to empty it and wipe it clean.

"And anyway he stopped," said Olof. "Sixteen times he cut her, and then he stopped."

He let his head and body fall back on to the pillow and mattress, and clasped his hands under his chin.

"What does he look like now?" he asked. "I've thought a lot about that, what he might look like. After all these years. Like last season's grass? Or like an ape? Or like a still-born calf?"

"Yes," she replied, "maybe that's what he looks like."

When she came back with the empty pail washed clean he was already asleep.

The wooden doll, the bit of wood that had presumably been a doll, was lying on the pillow beside Hadar. Part of it had turned black, because he had been in the habit of putting what must have been its head in his mouth and licking and sucking it.

"But in the end you left Minna in peace," she said to him, "after the sixteenth scar."

"Is that what Olof said?" he asked.

"Yes. That's what Olof says."

"So he counted!" Hadar said. "The bastard put his fingers there and counted!"

"She counted for him," she said. "She told him it was sixteen."

The winter outside was unvarying – no, not unvarying, it was encroaching further, the snow, the cold, probably even the darkness. Perhaps it was already January, perhaps Christmas had already passed. She hadn't celebrated Christmas since she was a child. For several days no paper had been delivered, so she was lighting the fire in the stove with strips of birch bark peeled off the firewood.

A Christmas card had arrived from Sundsvall, and she had fastened it to the wall with two drawing pins, next to the curtain by the dining table. Gustaf Adolfs Church in winter attire. All was well in Sundsvall. In front of the church door was a sketched-in Father Christmas with a lantern in his hand. Happy Christmas from your relations in Sundsvall!

"She was going to have a baby," said Hadar. "I didn't want to disturb the baby she had inside her."

He tried to raise his head and turn towards her, but despite his emaciation his skull was too heavy.

"So she had a child by you?" she said. "Minna had a child by you both?"

As he attempted to answer his face crumpled and his lips began to quiver so that he could scarcely get the words out.

"Yes," he said, "she bore a child right enough."

Then he lay still for a while gathering his strength.

"It was my child," he said.

And when his features had regained their composure he

explained to her what it was that had temporarily almost robbed him of his ability to speak, what it was that always affected him when his thoughts happened to stray to Minna and the child.

She should not imagine that it was his emotions that were getting the better of him. Emotions were an alien and unnatural and new-fangled concept. Emotions were something that people manufactured for themselves when they needed them, emotions were commodities or perhaps necessities that people made or produced when necessary. It was principally in crowds or larger communities that emotions could be of use, even between men, especially in southern Sweden. Emotions were tools that people employed to take command of themselves and others.

Up here emotions were of no use. He had never had any need for them; he had never even needed to be on his guard against them.

No, what went through him on those occasions when he could not prevent his thoughts going back to Minna and the child was something quite different from emotions, something immeasurably more potent and more malignant.

It was an internal tremor, a shaking and quaking that took his breath away and gripped his heart like the sound of a huge, powerful accordion. It was actually as if his whole ribcage, the whole of his insides, had taken on the form of a heaving, droning accordion. It was unendurable, it really was.

He knew of no name for the condition.

Yes, she gave birth to a child, a son, his, Hadar's son; that's what he should have been called, Hadarsson – he could have kept that name for posterity.

A male child who irrefutably bore his features and who had rosy cheeks and dark eyes and broad nails and strong wrists and who got deep furrows in his brow whenever his head was filled with thoughts.

Minna brought him over in the wicker basket to show him; he was only a few days old and she sat here in the kitchen and put him to her breast.

And he, Hadar, had lifted him up and held him in his hands and run his fingers over him to make sure his body was faultless and perfect.

And he had said to Minna that Edward was a good name, it was his paternal grandfather's name – the boy should be called Edward.

"Yes," Minna had said, "Edward is good, I like Edward. Edward is a pretty name."

But then Olof had taken the boy to the priest and had him christened Lars. He was never called Edward, only Lars. Lars had been their maternal grandfather in Sorsele whom none of them had ever seen; he had been run over by a railway wagon. "It's a dreadful thing," he said, "when a person isn't allowed to have his rightful name, when he's forced to live his life under the wrong name, when in one way he's himself, but in another is forced to be someone else.

"I can't go on any more for the moment," Hadar added. "You write your book now. I'll go to sleep."

DAYLIGHT LASTED ONLY A few hours; a sliver of sun showed itself fleetingly over the tops of the mountains to the south, then dawn turned slowly but inexorably into dusk.

It was during these hours of daylight that she went over to Olof. "Of course," he said one day, "of course you're staying with Hadar, it's his attic you're living in, but it's me that deep down you care about. You can't bear the thought of Hadar burying me, of him sinking me in the lake as if I were a stillborn calf, turning me into bait for the perch."

He even ventured to suggest that it was for his sake she had stayed on; she wanted to make sure he outlived Hadar. If there had been nothing here except for Hadar and his cancer, she would not have stayed on.

"I haven't stayed on," she said. "I'll be going almost any day now."

Then his voice turned whiny and plaintive and he reached out and touched her on the elbow. Did she mean that his life was not good enough, that it didn't provide sufficient reason for her to revise her travel plans completely and put aside all her other work, wasn't he an adequate and worthy object for her acts of charity, wasn't his life attractive and beautiful and of inestimable value?

"Your life is fine," she said.

During the last few weeks little red swellings had started to appear all over his body, particularly on his chest and shoulders. A rash, he said.

She bathed them with cold water and glycerine, having found the little bottle on one of the top shelves in the pantry. "That's Minna's glycerine," he said. "She used to put it on the lingonberries that went with the fish."

"Did you use to go fishing?" she asked. "In your boat, on the lake?"

"That was Minna's favourite sight," he said. "Someone in a boat on the lake. She would make up a lunch box, and then she'd say, 'Go and take the boat out on the lake'."

"And you ate the fish?"

"If you put a lot of sugar on perch, they're quite edible: they taste of marzipan. But there's nothing you can do with pike."

He added, "You eat fish with your finger and thumb."

It was a great disappointment for him, he went on, that she hadn't come to him long ago. He and she could have gone out together in the boat on the lake. He would have been many years younger – he would refrain from saying how many – he would have been stronger and more agile and more imaginative. Imagination had been his prime characteristic. Sugar on perch wasn't the only thing he had invented; there was also sweet turnip soup and the syrup you boil up from pine roots and sallow and the syrup you tap from willow, not to mention all the other things that he had devised and created and now forgotten. And his sweat had always smelt good, like soap or washing powder. His memory too was another reason why she should have found her way to him before: he had had an outstanding and faultless memory. But it was beginning to fail him now, both his memory and long complex trains of thought. He could remember quite clearly the way his thoughts had linked up to each other, one after another, like the vertebrae of a fish.

In those days she could have asked him about anything.

He ought perhaps to mention that he had once known exactly what death was like and eternity and God. He really could have answered any questions at all. But now he had forgotten everything. He could not remember anything of his thoughts or his knowledge. Not having come long ago, she would never get from him now any reliable answers to the big questions in life.

But he could still remember perfectly well how clearly he had known everything. That memory, which strictly speaking was more a kind of forgetfulness, was as good as any faith; in fact that was what constituted his steadfast belief.

"That's as certain as can be," he said.

In the centre of each of the red swellings on his chest and arms little white pustules had begun to appear.

"The rash is producing syrup," he said.

"Anyway, why would I have come to you with my questions?" she asked.

On loneliness, a subject she brought up on several occasions, Hadar had this to say:

The best thing about a solitary life was that you really got to know yourself. You didn't have to make an effort to try to understand anyone else, you could direct all your powers of thought inwards into yourself. Now, he ventured to maintain, there was nothing within him that was unknown to him.

What he hated most of all in others was any kind of self-deception. He had never lied to himself. He was his own judge, a very stern judge. If he had a fault, that was it: he was far too merciless towards himself, even almost cruel at times.

As in the case of urges and desires. He had rebuked himself with such severity in that respect that his desires had sometimes been turned into their opposite and had become a cross that he had to bear.

But on the whole things were good.

What he most prized in himself was his love of the truth. He was incapable of falsehood.

He had to admit that he hated himself for being honest; but he also took pride and pleasure in his capacity for honesty. He had loved even the hardest and most hateful truths. He had begged and pleaded with the doctor to show him the photograph of his tumour; indeed, had it been possible he would have liked it to be excised and put in a glass jar so that he could keep it constantly before his eyes. That had been his attitude to all the deformities and abscesses and wounds in his life; he had wanted to keep them perpetually before his eyes.

He prided himself too on never interfering in the lives of others, he always left them in peace.

"And that's the truth," he said.

Whereas Olof, on the other hand, would be drowned and destroyed by his deceitfulness and mendacity.

If she had come at a different time of year, she said to Hadar, if it hadn't been for this abominable winter, she wouldn't have stayed even as fleetingly as she was now doing; she wouldn't so thoughtlessly have allowed herself even a night or two. She was sure she wouldn't have indulged in this little break.

"You've got to be somewhere," he replied.

When she went on to ask him about the boy – no, not asked about but just mentioned the little fellow that Minna had carried and given birth to and who had not been allowed to bear his right name, the child Minna had brought in the wicker basket – then he started talking about his pain, his voice quavering as he rapped his knuckles against his forehead and temples.

She must understand, he said, if he was not able to converse with her as readily and easily as she might have expected, if he could not make small talk about this and that as was probably usual in southern Sweden, but it was just that the pain kept on interrupting his thoughts and speech. It was like a clock striking, the pain was, and you had to stop talking and count the strokes; or like a woodpecker taking a moment's rest before resuming its frenzied drilling.

Olof was not subject to pain, of course. He could talk for ever about anything without interruption, pausing only to draw breath from time to time. There was no room for pain in such a sweet life as his. There was however a mysterious connection between pain and savoury things, pain was in some ways the ultimate form of saltiness.

It also made him agitated, the pain that is, in which he included his suffering and affliction and torment – the pain and the agitation both stemmed from the tumour.

He would like to imagine that it was still only a single tumour, that was why he just said the tumour: the original tumour so to speak, the one he had almost managed to get used to and learn to live with. Even if it had now bred and given rise to countless progeny, suckers and shoots in the strangest places inside his body, he preferred to hold on in his thoughts to the first and definitely genuine tumour. That also kept the pain whole and indivisible.

It would be excruciating, or unnecessarily stressful anyway, to imagine a tangle or log-jam of subsidiary pains and referred pain that his mind would have to struggle in vain to distinguish and formulate a clear impression of.

Of course it could not be denied that pain, if you really searched your heart, consisted of innumerable springs and tributaries that finally joined together in one great watercourse flooding through your whole body – but that was of little significance for your own personal experience of pain.

Olof, he pointed out, would never be able to talk to her like this; he had never experienced pain, he was not even ill, just dying.

"He is dying, isn't he?" he asked.

"Yes," she said. "He seems to be in the process of dying."

Pain was uncommon up here, he went on. At any rate, you seldom saw it. He could not remember ever having seen any pain to speak of among his friends or relations, despite the fact that they had obviously been ill or even died in his presence. Perhaps there had been pain present, but he had never caught sight of it. Perhaps the cold and the snow and the darkness had a painkilling effect.

He understood that down south pain was very much more common and also given more attention.

That was why he was so pleased, or at least found it some comfort, that she had decided to make this journey for his sake and stay with him. Since she was from the south he could talk to her completely openly, almost flippantly, about pain; he didn't need to hide it from her – for her, pain was the most natural thing in the world.

Everyone, he thought, should be allowed to have a person from southern Sweden by his side at the end, a person who could accept pain without embarrassment, even completely unaffected, and cope with all the moaning and groaning.

The final pains in life were indescribably arduous; they were not just themselves, they also contained traces and elements of countless pains from the past. They were thick with the impurities of all the deposits that were stirred up from the bottom of your life. His head really wasn't big enough for the pains he had to experience and think about. On the one hand the pain exhausted him to the point where he just wanted to sleep for eternity, and on the other hand it kept him awake. For the first part of his time in death he would just rest, then he would see.

At long last he did actually have a few words to say about the boy Minna had borne him.

"He grew up," he said. "He grew up and became a big lad."

On another occasion she asked Hadar:

"Who will have all your things when you've gone? When you eventually die?"

"Not Olof!"

"No. But when you've inherited from Olof and built the sauna and then die yourself?"

"No one!"

"No one? But what about the forest and the house and the firewood and the outhouses?"

"No. No one."

"That won't do," she said. "There has to be someone."

"It can go back."

"Go back?"

"It can revert to nature," he said. "It can go back to how it was before."

"That I don't understand," she said.

So he tried to make himself clear. It should go back to its original state; what he imagined was a reversion in which everything human and unnatural was slowly erased. It would sink down into the new undergrowth and the forest would take over. It would still be there, but so unobtrusive and hidden that no one would notice it.

"It will be owned by no one," he said.

"You're freezing," said Olof one day. "Your nose is blue and your hands are chapped."

She admitted it, she was freezing, and she had felt frozen on every one of these few and still easily reckonable days that she had tarried in Övreberg. The hardest to bear, she said, were the mild days with a strong wind.

"You're too skimpily dressed," he said.

"I don't live here," she replied. "I don't have to be dressed for the weather up here."

"You can wear some of Minna's clothes," he said. "You can take what you want out of Minna's wardrobe."

She had never opened the door of the blue-painted cupboard in the bedroom before. Inside, it smelt of old wool and mothballs. She found a thick grey cardigan, out at the elbows, and a heavy black coat made of some kind of coarse homespun cloth.

When she tried them on in the kitchen Olof said, "It's like seeing Minna again, Minna going to fetch the post or taking the kick-sledge and going out to the road to watch the cars go by."

But then he went on to say that she wasn't pale enough. No, she didn't have the requisite whiteness about her. If you could remove the colour in her cheeks and her eyebrows and make her hair chalky white, then she would be perfect, only then would she be as ineffably pretty as Minna had been.

She had also found a pair of red tasselled mittens in the wardrobe.

Hadar too recognised the cardigan and coat.

"Everything repeats itself," he said. "You never see the last of anything. At the end all you see around you are reminders and recurrences and resemblances and repetitions."

From then on she mostly went around in those clothes, Minna's clothes. They seemed made for the changeable weather and Övreberg.

Perhaps the worst of the winter was already over anyway. Although there was snow still falling some days and the stove had to be stoked up every evening, in the middle of the day the sun was now completely visible for an hour or so, and the snow on the roof had started to thaw, the droplets forming thin glistening runnels down the windows.

She told Olof about Hadar's suffering.

"Good," he said. "Good."

Because presumably the worse the pains got, the closer to death he was.

"Yes," she said. "I suppose that's the case."

He for his part had this predominant illness, his heart, he

said, and that in turn had its secondary ailments like the swellings on his chest and arms, besides which he had minor aches and spasms and infirmities that hardly deserved mention by name, ranging right down to itches and tingles, causing discomfort for the most part, though at times quite enjoyable. But pain, no – even the word was alien and repellent to him.

There was nothing, he thought, to suggest that he was approaching death. There were some days when he could actually imagine that life felt more agreeable and more secure. There was no longer anything he need worry about; he could direct all his energies to simply existing, whole-heartedly and without restraint. Every day that passed brought him closer to victory over Hadar. Before he went to sleep at night he would clasp his hands under his chin and heave a deep sigh of pure and serene gratitude.

"What's that spoon for?" she asked.

He was clutching a teaspoon in his right hand, as if trying to conceal it from her.

"It's just a spoon," he said. "A teaspoon."

He was holding it in his palm, the way Hadar held the wooden doll. The handle was made of yellow bone and the bowl of the spoon was grey, presumably aluminium.

He looked at the water trickling down the window. She was not to imagine, he remarked, that it would soon be spring and summer just because the odd little bit of snow was melting; this thaw was nothing but lies and deception – the idea was to lure us into fortitude. If there was never a mild spell nor a glimpse of sun people would succumb to feelings of misery and despair.

For many, spring and summer seemed to constitute the meaning of life. It was depressing to think of the joy they apparently derived from watching something as insignificant as these drops of water on a window pane.

The seasons left him unmoved and indifferent himself. He had managed to rise above the absurdity and predictability of such changes. He was quite indifferent now to all the silly little things in life. That was a virtue, but he could claim no credit for it, he had merely given in to it.

"I can wash up the teaspoon for you," she said.

But washing up and cleaning were also futile vanities that he had now put behind him.

Whatever slight impurity and tiny amount of contagious matter there might be on a teaspoon was hardly going to bother him. A wasted and skeletal body like Hadar's was more vulnerable and exposed, of course. There was no protective sheath round an emaciated person. But he himself was clothed in flesh that could keep out most kinds of infection and contagion.

And furthermore the teaspoon was his, nothing to do with her! He had his own reasons for just wanting to hold it in his hand.

She had to admit that the teaspoon, whether washed up or not, was hardly of any great significance.

But he nevertheless wanted her to see his clever and ingenious use of the teaspoon.

He did it with precision and care, looking up at her from time to time, proudly and secretively.

He felt over his chest with the fingertips of his left hand, and when he found a large boil crowned by a full pustule, he carefully scratched a hole in the skin with his fingernail. Then he scraped out the liquid from the burst pustule with his teaspoon. It was slightly viscous, but as clear as water.

Then he put the teaspoon to his lips and sucked and licked it dry.

"It's like honey," he said.

Three pimples, he had discovered, gave him a teaspoonful. He had thought up the method himself. If you're lying on your back day in and day out, anything can happen. That was what the alchemists had done in the past, they had lain on their backs for days on end with their brains seething. There were generative powers within him that no one, not even himself, could have envisaged. Perhaps in the end he would be able to produce all the sweetness and nourishment he needed on his own.

Would she like to taste it?

"No thank you," she said.

This syrup or nectar was also natural and unrefined, so it was probably healthier than all the food available in the shops. Perhaps in the end it would even make him well.

And the pimples healed over in no time at all; he could milk them again after a couple of hours.

He would remind her of what he had said earlier about illness: it wasn't as unambiguous and uncomplicated as you might at first think. It was primarily evil, of course, and not merely evil but excruciatingly painful and hellish, but it also had its good aspects, its own fruitfulness, its attractive side effects and its own cycle.

"Do you believe me?"

"I can't say I believe you. But I can see that it's true."

Now there were even a few weak rays of sun shining in through the window. When she had helped him with his daily tasks she said, "You could have had someone to do all this for you."

"I've got you," he said.

"No, you haven't," she said. "I've only done it because you haven't got anyone else."

"And who could there have been?" he asked.

"The son that Minna bore you," she said. "Lars."

"Never," he said. "That's not the sort of person he was."

No, his son was certainly not that sort! He was much too splendid and precious a lad, much too broad-shouldered and gifted to be put to work of that kind! He had to laugh when he thought of his son emptying his pail or wiping his bottom! His son who would go on to be a schoolteacher or priest or surveyor or the kind of person who would write books about the solar system or frogs, whose skin would be as pale and delicate as paper! No, never!

"You're not using his name," she said.

"His name?"

"You're not saying it," she said.

But why should he use his name when it would have no effect? When his son couldn't come running if he called his name?

Why should he use a name that meant nothing to anyone, why should he say the name to her when she could not even imagine for a moment what the boy looked like when he came striding into the kitchen with a pike he had snared – no, not the boy but the young man with the blue-flecked eyes and stubble on his chin?

She could use his name as much and as often as she wanted, but it would never pass his lips.

"But he was called Lars?"

"Yes. He was called Lars."

*

That evening – or it might have been several weeks later – Hadar asked again whether she really sat at her table writing every evening.

"I don't think you're getting down to it as you should," he said. "I think you're too comfortable here with me. I think you're the sort of person who just lets the days drift by."

"I am writing," she replied.

"I can never be sure of that," he said. "I can never be sure of anything. What you're doing up in the bedroom. I lie here and you lie there."

So she fetched her writing pad and read him the page she had written the previous evening. Her gruff and rasping voice emphasised the dryness of the text as she sat on the chair at the foot of the sofa and read to him.

". . . no longer conceivable nowadays, words that had been obliterated or were possibly to be regarded as a memorial to earlier times when there was still thought to be a clear connection between the will and the act, figures of speech as expressions of reverence, a faded respectful memory upon which to dwell. But the primary characteristic of St Christopher is not obedience; the concept of obedience has no place at all in the world of ideas to which St Christopher belongs. Nor can one speak of submission: he does not subject himself to a divine order or a holy calling; it is not love or goodness or even sympathy for his fellow human beings that motivates or drives him. It would be vain to attempt to interpret his actions, or rather his obsession, his passionate single-mindedness, in ethical or moral terms.

"It is his existence rather than his words that speak for him.

"If he were suddenly to announce: 'I'm giving up now, I'm going home', what would we think? No, St Christopher, as he manifests himself in this account, could never utter such an absurd, discordant and offensive remark. For him a home would be unthinkable; if he had a home he would not exist in his capacity of St Christopher, a home would expunge him. Any particular direction or geographically definable goal for his travelling is basically beyond the bounds of possibility; his goal has to remain obscure and presumptuously speculative and transcendental; his mission necessarily the unattainable.

"The only rule to which he conforms is that of representation, that universal and eternally binding model to which the rest of humanity is also unknowingly subject. His representative function is neither willing nor unwilling, he simply performs it.

"What he represents is a matter of fundamental indifference to him. He probably has a vague awareness from time to time that he represents mankind and his burdens, the giant who can never have enough to carry, the divine vehicle, the bearer of burdens who is only sated when he shoulders the Lord of Creation, and so on. But his prime object remains the representative function. If one can speak of a prime object in respect of St Christopher. In all probability the concept of prime object must be expressed and read here with contemplative irony; anything else would be to ascribe to the figure or image/model of St Christopher a lack of ambiguity that would be insulting, even fatal for his independence and uniqueness. If it were possible in the sphere of the holy and the divine to use such irony, it might even be possible to call St Christopher obedient. Even a word like piety . . ."

"Ah yes," said Hadar. "Obedient, he certainly was."

"Who?" she asked. "Who was obedient?"

But the question was superfluous – he was obviously talking about his son, his and Minna's son, maybe Olof's son too!

Yes, he had been obedient, he had never been obstinate or difficult, he had always done what he was told, and the bigger and older and more sensible he got, the more useful and obedient he proved to be. Pious, certainly, that's what he had been. "Yes, I'll do it" was the only answer he was capable of giving, and everything he was asked to do he had done with a smile, and often with a song on his lips. He was a stubborn and persistent worker – though he used to straighten up from time to time to flick his hair out of his eyes – and he was left-handed, but that was no disability.

"What I've written," she asked, "what I just read out, was it intelligible?"

"Oh yes," said Hadar, "I understood every word."

And he continued speaking about his son:

Yes, he had been obedient in everything: in his speech, in his deeds, right down to the tiniest movement and gesture.

And he, Hadar, had bought him the guitar, the guitar with six strings and a strap of blue webbing to go round his neck, and he had practised playing over at Olof's place, Olof's house that he occasionally and absent-mindedly called home, and then, when he had learnt to play properly, he had come and made music here in his house, here in the kitchen, in his, Hadar's, kitchen. And he had had ruddy cheeks and blue eyes, nothing like Minna's chalk-white skin and pink eyes. It had been a miracle to see a person like him here on earth. What a son to have! Ah, having the best horse or the most impressive home was nothing compared to having a son like that!

"My eyes are sore," he added. "That's why they're red and watery."

"I can get your car started," she said to Hadar later. "I can dig it out of the snow."

"What would be the point of that?" he asked.

"If I speak to the doctor in the village about your pains, he'll be able to give you something stronger."

"I'm all right," he said. "I'm not bothered about my insides any longer."

"You can't lie still any more," she said. "And you can't sit down either. You need help."

"I've got all the help I need," he said. "And Olof isn't taking any painkillers."

"He's not in pain."

"It makes no difference. When he's dead you can go and get as many pills and drops as you like."

When that time came, when Olof was gone and done with, then he would take nothing but painkillers, he would gorge himself on painkillers and he would wash everything down with glass after glass of painkiller, horehound and willow bark and red and white and yellow pills, and she could get syringes and tubes and stuff him full of painkillers.

But while Olof was still alive . . .

Yes, that's how it was for him as he grew up, his son – he had been son and heir in both places, and both had been his home.

Hadar could also remember that he had brought up the

subject – the boy himself, that is – he'd tried to talk to him, Hadar, about how they got on with one another, that it was actually his great good fortune to have them both, to have not just one of them but both of them. Having not only Olof but Hadar too, having not only Hadar but Olof. If he couldn't go to one of them, he could go to the other. He could go to one as well as the other. Like when he was nearly grown up, being an adult and needing a moped, and when he wanted a leather jacket with a high collar, and dark red shoes with pointed toes, and a fishing rod with a line that would never tangle.

"How much does it cost?" Hadar had asked.

"What?" the boy replied.

"The leather jacket."

"Two hundred crowns."

"Here you are," Hadar had said.

But it had its drawbacks too. It was hard for the boy to get his mind round it, he felt a peculiar conflict deep inside, it seemed impossible for him to combine them into one coherent whole, Hadar and Olof, to keep them both in his mind at the same time. He would first think of one and then the other. And when he thought of Olof he felt full of certain qualities and characteristics, and when he thought of Hadar he became a totally different person.

Hadar had said, "I can understand perfectly well that you can't talk to Olof about that."

He wanted to be indivisible, he had said; his only wish was to feel at one within himself.

"You're like a veneer pine," Hadar had said. "You're like the rootstock of an eighteen-inch thick pine."

But to get Hadar to understand, he had told him about

the time he had gone out on the ice and nearly drowned.

"You nearly drowned?" Hadar had exclaimed. "Nobody told me!"

That was just as well, the boy had said, since Hadar would only have worried, and by the time there was a chance to tell him it was already over.

"You never know," Hadar had said, "for you I could perform miracles."

It had been that same winter, when they had been out on the ice, he and the other boys the school was going to turn into magistrates and foresters and teachers and vets. He had gone out a bit too far and fallen through a hole in the ice.

"I'm not sure," Hadar had said, "that I can bear to hear this."

And as he fell through the hole he went down so swiftly that he was carried along in the water, away from the edge of the ice and the daylight. He had immediately thrashed out and started swimming; it would not be an overstatement to say that he had swum as if his life depended on it.

Hadar recalled that as he had listened to the boy telling him this his whole body had started shaking and he had had to lie down on the sofa.

So the boy had swum around down there beneath the ice, striking his knuckles and head and shoulders on its rough, sharp underside, trying to find his way back to the ice hole. Or another ice hole. In his memory it was as if he had swum around under water holding his breath for an hour or more, but in reality of course it can have been only about a minute. And all the time, for the whole of that endless minute, he had thought about his long, almost fifteen-year, life. He had thought of Minna. And he had strained himself to the utmost to think of them both at the same time, Olof and Hadar. In his desperation he had wanted to link them both together into one being whom he could call to or at least send a last thought to. But it had been impossible. However much he strained his mind he had not been able to unite them. Hadar had remained Hadar and Olof Olof. He had finally given up; he had thrown out the one and kept the other in his thoughts, and the very moment he did so he found the ice hole again and stuck his head through and drew breath. Whether it was the same hole or a different one was impossible to say, since he himself was no longer the same.

And Hadar had been so totally exhausted from hearing all this that he did not even have the strength left to ask the boy which of them he had rejected and which he had kept.

"And how much does the fishing rod cost?" he had asked instead.

"A hundred and fifty crowns," the boy had replied.

"Here you are then," Hadar had said.

Sometimes they would talk about what they missed, both Hadar and Olof. Paths in the forest and the lapping of the water against the sides of the boat and animals slaughtered long ago and bumblebee nests in the grass and lingonberry juice and thunderstorms and bathing their feet in a cold spring. And Hadar remembered raw seagulls' eggs.

But worst of all, he said, or nearly worst, was missing Minna.

Or not exactly Minna, but Minna all the same. He had never had anyone else. After her he had had nobody. It was dreadful not having anyone at all. In actual fact he had not really had Minna, of course – she had by no means been indivisibly his. With Minna things had been the way they were, he and she had not had just each other, but he had had her nevertheless.

And he had had nobody before her. There had been a great emptiness both before and after Minna. Especially after her.

Until his dying day he would miss what he and Minna had done together, he would miss it for the rest of his life.

"What you mean," she said, "is that you miss a woman, that you need a woman."

She should not misrepresent what he said so crassly and so outrageously. It was unbelievable that she could speak so crudely and immodestly, though it was much as he would expect from a person from down south. In the south there was no sense of decency or respectability or chastity. He wanted to make it clear that he was hurt and upset by her words.

"You ought to be ashamed of yourself!" he said.

"I could help you," she said.

"How?" he asked. "How could you help me?"

"With my hand," she said. "With my hand, the way a woman does with a man."

"I don't know anything about that," he said. "But if you say so."

So she undid his clothes and took his yellowing shrunken member in her hand and rubbed it and squeezed it until it half raised itself, talking to him softly and soothingly as she did so: the ploughman will go forth in March and turn the same soil he has always turned, and the birds will sing their same song – until finally he gave a deep and anguished groan and the palm of her hand was filled with semen.

It was grey-green in colour, with a strong odour of ammonia and maybe even of mould.

He lifted his head to see it and sniff it; she held out her hand.

"Ah," he said, "that sperm looks like pus or venom. But it could be thirty years old. Or forty."

"Well, I know next to nothing about sperm myself," she said.

Olof would often say, "I can always manage."

Sometimes he said, "I get by remarkably well."

Or occasionally, "It's thanks to the incomprehensible grace of God that I get on so well."

One day she asked, "How long is this duel going to continue? How long will you both last out? How long will Hadar wait for you and how long will you wait for Hadar?"

"For ever," Olof replied. "There's no given time limit. And spring will be here any moment."

He was sucking on a fig and smacking his lips as he spoke the words. Or rather, two figs, one in each cheek.

"After that it will soon be summer," he went on. "And you don't die in summer. I never would, and Hadar is hardly likely to. It's like the Garden of Eden up here then, on the stones and gravel round the lake. The rowan trees and birch and dandelions and lemmings. No, I can't see anything coming to an end."

Then he tried once more to persuade her to taste the juice that he was scraping out of the pustules on his chest.

She explained that she had always found bodily fluids repulsive, other people's bodily fluids; there was something private and intimate about bodily fluids that disgusted her. She also thought that he himself needed all the nourishment he could get.

102

But, he objected, this was no bodily fluid in the usual meaning of the phrase. He was more inclined to call it nectar or sap or juice, its sources mysterious but nonetheless natural.

She tried to turn the conversation to something else. "Your contentment," she said, "is a great resource for you. You can still take pleasure in life. Everything has gone well for you, I can't think of anybody who would not have reason to envy you your life."

"Yes," he said. "That's certainly true."

By now the fir trees at the foot of the hill were free of snow most of the time. They stood out black against the ice-covered lake. But every so often it would snow again, usually in the afternoons. As they talked now more snow was falling, the heavy flakes clinging to the window panes.

"That's certainly true," he repeated. "But there's one thing I regret. There's one thing I'll regret to the end of my days."

Perhaps the word regret was far too weak, he mused, even remorse was inadequate; the only word for it, a word which was too cumbersome and too grand for his simple lips, was contrition. It was that regret, not to say contrition, that he had frequently – no, constantly – sought some kind of remedy for, or at least a moment or two of forgetfulness.

"It's not possible to do anything up here that's worth regretting, is it?" she asked.

"How would you know?" he asked.

"What is it that you regret?"

"Making him dig that ditch," he said. "Not letting him go down to the creek and snare pike. Making him dig that big ditch."

"Who?" she asked. "Who did you make do it?"

"Lars." Had she forgotten him, his son, his and Minna's son?

"You didn't want to talk about him," she said.

"Really and truly I never want to talk about anyone else," Olof said. "Without him there's no one worth talking about."

"What ditch?" she asked. "Where did you make him dig?"

"Between Hadar's cottage and mine," he said. "A deep ditch that no one would be able to jump over."

"There isn't any ditch," she said. "I walk along there every day and I don't see any ditch."

But he did not want to talk about the ditch any more; he shut his eyes and clasped his hands under his chin.

"I want to go to sleep," he said. "Never left in peace. It's a blessing that you're looking after me, but you must leave me in peace as well."

And he added, "It's like this, you see: when you've lived a long time, in the end your experience and intellect and memories become so extensive that anything, and I mean anything, might ooze or squirt out of you if you're prodded carelessly. People should be left in peace."

It was becoming increasingly difficult to shave Hadar; the bristles of his beard seemed to be getting coarser and tougher with every day that passed, as if they were ossifying, as if they were growing directly out of the skull. She had to strop the razor time and time again.

"We can't go on like this," she said. "I'll have to bring the situation to an end in one way or another."

"You could kill Olof," Hadar said.

"Summer is coming," she said. "Spring and then summer. And no one dies during the summer."

"So summer's on the way?" said Hadar.

"I don't know," she said. "But Olof says it is. How would I be able to recognise summer up here?"

"You'll recognise it when you see it. The rowans in blossom and the lemmings and the birch and the dandelions and the smell of the bog-myrtle. If you can't recognise summer, you might as well be a burbot or a field-mouse or an earthworm."

Whenever she nicked him with the razor now no blood appeared, nor even any water; the white of flesh and bone was exposed, that was all.

As she stropped the razor yet again she continued talking to him – about his condition and about the situation that needed to be fundamentally changed.

It really was essential that he should finally pull himself together and die; he shouldn't begrudge himself that freedom – after all, he was a free man.

This clinging on to life was a form of slavery, slavery to Olof; he was letting Olof rule over him to the last breath. Since man has reason he is free; free will is the cause of our actions – if not the primary then at least the secondary or tertiary cause.

Letting yourself die was an action. He must act in accordance with his reason, otherwise he would have completely given up his freedom.

"When I'm dead," said Hadar, "I won't be free any more. When I'm dead, I'll be deaf and blind and dumb. But Olof, he'll be lying there alive, with the freedom to do whatever comes into his head, risky ventures and exciting journeys and crazy schemes."

"Olof is as unfree as you are," she said.

But he didn't believe that, he denied it categorically; he

wasn't concerned about that, he didn't think that Olof's heart was impaired in the slightest – it was just a bit confined and fettered and constricted in all the fat.

He was sorry that she accepted Olof's notions and absurdities so easily, that she actually bothered to listen to him when he held forth. It was a damned nuisance that she had to go down there and look after him every day; he wished there were some insuperable barrier blocking her way to Olof, that there were no path between the two houses.

If only the embankment had been built as intended, then she would never even have found out that Olof existed.

"What embankment?" she asked.

Why, was this something new that she hadn't heard already?

It wasn't possible, they couldn't have been living together for as long as they had, he and she, without him having told her about the embankment!

What he was talking about, of course, was the high – the immense – bank of earth between his house and Olof's, the bank that no one would be able to jump or climb over, the bulwark or wall that would shut people in on the right side, or on the wrong side if that was their last wish, his son and Minna and even the guitar for that matter. There would finally be an end to all the coming and going: they would have to decide who they belonged to, him or Olof. People have to make a choice, that's what they have to do, they have to choose. And the top of the wall was to have been crowned with barbed wire and broken bottles.

"You can simply go round a wall like that," she said.

"Not if it stretches from the cliff by Storgrova right down to the lake."

"Olof mentioned a ditch," she said. "A ditch between your house and his."

Hadar put the wooden doll in his mouth every now and again and sucked on it.

A ditch, but of course, if there was a bank there was also a ditch. When his son dug out the earth and the stones and the rocks and piled it all up, a ditch appeared; the ditch was the result of the embankment, a result and a prerequisite; the material had to come from somewhere – if you build an embankment you also dig a ditch. But the aim was to build the embankment, not to dig the ditch.

"And it was your son who dug and built, your and Minna's son, or Olof's?"

"Him and me," said Hadar. "Though he was the one who dug and pickaxed and shovelled."

He, his son, had been nearly sixteen, and was at home from the school that was going to make a magistrate or a forester of him. It was spring and summer and he just had his blue trousers and boots on; he was a joy to behold. He had dug and shovelled till the sweat ran off him. He was fired with enthusiasm for the project, but had not indicated where he would eventually stay, which side of the embankment he would choose.

But it was likely there had been some unspoken agreement between them, Hadar and his son.

And Hadar had usually stood watching him, giving advice and instructions, where the pickaxe should go under the rocks, how the stones and earth should be piled up so as not to slither down – he had been like a field-marshal. As far as he could recall, those days had been the happiest in his life.

He broke off there; he came to a halt at the happiest days of his life.

Then he said, "You won't desert me, will you?"

"Desert?" she replied. "You can only do that if you belong together."

"Couldn't you play the zither to me?" he asked.

But that she couldn't do, she couldn't play the zither.

"Hadar says that it wasn't a ditch that was to be dug," she said to Olof, "but an embankment that was to be built."

"The boy had to put it somewhere, the earth that he dug up out of the ditch," Olof said, "so it turned into an embankment. If you dig a ditch you get an embankment."

"And he doesn't think there's anything wrong with your heart."

To which Olof replied, suddenly and unexpectedly, "Well, it may be so, he could well be right, could Hadar."

Of course he had to justify the confession: his illness was not really anything to talk about, it was a source of annoyance, nothing else, but the mere thought of the illness, his heart, was a torment to him; the very thought of it was a worse torment than the illness itself, his heart itself.

His so-called illness was nothing special; no, frankly it was quite ordinary. And his heart was actually not weak; in all probability it was simply too strong. It was its violent and furious strength that was its weak point. It hammered and pounded so hard against his ribs from inside that he feared they might crack. Yes, his unbridled heart had completely taken control of him, but apart from that he was healthier than he had ever been.

"Whereas actually," she said, "it would be easy to get the impression that you're at death's door."

"No, far from it!"

He had been lying still and resting for almost a whole year now. That rest could not fail to have an effect; rest was the only thing that helped against the worst trials and tribulations. He was getting stronger with every day that passed, and eventually the day would come when he was completely rested, and then everything would be over.

She asked where the guitar was now.

"What guitar?"

"The one the boy used to play."

Ah, yes. He had quite forgotten that. It would have been silly and pointless for him to have remembered anyway, but it had existed and the boy had fooled around with it once or twice. He had tried to get some tunes out of it but never really succeeded.

Now thank goodness it had been burnt; now that no one had any reason to play it, it had been burnt. He had forgotten that. A guitar that no one played, a cheap and insignificant bargain-basement guitar, might just as well be burnt.

"You're not sweating any more," she said to Hadar. "You told me a long time ago that you were going to sweat yourself back to health."

"A long time ago?" he said. "That's hardly possible. You've only just come. I've only recently fetched you here."

"It's all too long ago," she said. "When I arrived, your cat was still alive."

That made him try to turn his head towards the door to see whether the cat really was gone.

"But what about him?" he asked. "Was he still here? My son?"

"No," she said. "I've never seen him."

No, of course, he knew that; he was embarrassed and ashamed at his absent-mindedness. The illness had probably attacked even his memory now, the illness in conjunction with the winter cold; his memory had always been better in the summer than the winter, when everything froze.

He rubbed his forehead and scalp with both hands to thaw his frozen thoughts and memories inside his ice-cold head.

No, of course she could never have seen his son, no one could have seen his son for years, not since that spring when the embankment was being built, he knew that perfectly well. If only Olof hadn't been there, and that contraption that he built! The lifting contraption that he made from four tree trunks, with a boom and a winch and a chain! The timber hoist by means of which he heaved up the blocks of stone and tree roots!

"Who?" she asked. "Who built the contraption?"

"My son, of course!"

No one in this part of the country but his son could have achieved such a thing, such a magnificent invention, no one but his son with his sinewy arms and clear mind!

And at that instant he remembered the birthmark: he had had a birthmark on his right shoulder that looked like a butterfly, and when he flexed his muscles the butterfly appeared to flutter.

"And the chain was from the log rafts," he added.

Then he fell silent.

"Yes?" she prompted. "And?"

But he could remember no more for the moment, he had

floated up to the surface of all the years he had lived and he could remember nothing more.

That's what he was like now. He even said it himself sometimes, "That's what I'm like now."

Occasionally he would point to something with the fingers he could no longer straighten out and ask, "What's that?"

"That's the special contraption you fixed to the wall," she answered.

Beside Olof's kitchen window there was a picture from a newspaper, brown with age, hanging from a drawing pin; it was impossible to see what it depicted.

One day when she happened to be standing in front of it, Olof said, "You mustn't take that away!"

"What?" she asked.

"The picture from the paper," he said. "It must stay where it is."

"I wasn't going to take it away," she said. "But it's not a picture any more."

"There's no finer picture," he said. "Minna cut it out and fastened it up. From the North Västerbothnian."

"What was it of?" she asked.

"It's the summer of fifty-nine," he said, "spring fifty-nine."

That's what it was. He could see every detail in the picture before him: the hill going down towards Arnberg Sound, the two big birch trees, the ferry on its way across the water, the Risliden ferry, the willow bushes down by the shore, the nineteenth of May fifty-nine, the man carrying the fish trap on his shoulder – Minna thought it looked like Lambert Ekman – and the air was mild and sweet-smelling from the grass and the rising sap.

The summer of fifty-nine.

It had been the last real summer; since then there had been only unseasonal summers and phantom summers, mock summers and illusory summers.

"Ah, you must remember that spring?"

But she had no memory of any particular spring. As far as she was aware, they were all the same.

It was that spring and summer when the ditch was to be dug, the big ditch, and events took the turn they did, and now he was lying here and everything was all right as far as it went, but nothing had been the same since, after fifty-nine. He was weak and abandoned, not half dead but only half alive, and now she was the only person he had, she who claimed to be his carer and yet wouldn't even taste the juice he got from the boils on his chest.

So finally she gave in and let him empty the teaspoon into the palm of her hand and she licked up the few drops.

"It reminds me of something," she said. "But I can't place it."

It was the same for him, he declared. For some reason that he couldn't understand this taste always made him think of his and Minna's boy. Which was strange and inexplicable because he had never in any way tasted the boy – in these latitudes you didn't do that sort of thing.

It might possibly, however, have something to do with the taste he had had in his mouth that time when he was doing his utmost to save the boy, when he was fighting like a wild animal to keep him, that time in the summer of fifty-nine when he got his mouth full of blood and was spitting out sweet mucus and watery blood for at least three days afterwards.

Then he brought the conversation to a close.

"It's all connected," he said. "The picture on the wall and the taste on my tongue and the summer of fifty-nine and the boy. They're all connected."

And he added, "Fancy you tasting it after all! I never thought you would!"

The stores they had built up for themselves in the outhouses and bedrooms and attics seemed inexhaustible: food, sweets, drinks, painkillers.

"You scarcely use anything," she said to Hadar. "And it's the same with Olof."

"I might have a long time to go," he said. "And Olof nearly as long."

"You don't take time seriously," she said. "You just let it go by, and hardly even that. You don't go along with it, you don't subject yourselves to it."

He was chewing one of the strong white tablets; swallowing was becoming increasingly difficult for him.

"When anything really happens," he said, "it's always fast. When something happens, it doesn't matter whether you're walking or sitting or lying, you're completely helpless. That's how it was with the boy and that's how it was with Minna. That's how it is."

"I don't know anything about it," she said. "About the boy and Minna."

No – no, she never knew anything. She was always ignorant. At least that was what she wanted him to think, that everything was unfamiliar to her.

But this was what had happened, he must tell her anyway: the boy had erected the timber construction by the embankment that was to be built; he had secured the chain round a rock that was the shape of a horse's head, an enormous horse's head, and he had hoisted the rock in the air, and there it hung on the chain.

That was when it happened.

And no one but Minna saw it. She had taken a kitchen chair outside and was sitting in the shade beneath the rowan tree. She had her sunglasses on to protect her from the light, and was sitting reading the North Västerbothnian and keeping an eye on the boy at the same time. She always seemed to be expecting something to happen; that's the sort of person she was.

It was something that happened to the rock, or something that happened to the chain or the winch.

This was in the summer of fifty-nine.

The chain whipped back on itself and made a loop, and the loop caught the boy under one arm and round his neck so that he was swept up into the air and left hanging, and the rock came crashing down to the ground.

"It surprises me," Hadar said, "that I've got the energy to tell you all this."

To which he added, "And it wasn't the easiest thing to tell you about."

He had swallowed his tablet.

"You don't have to," she said. "You can have a rest."

But he wanted to finish what he'd started, she should finally hear what Olof was really like. And time, he went on, can to some extent be resisted, whereas you can never defend yourself against events.

As far as this event was concerned, when the boy was yanked up in the air and hanged by the chain, it was only Minna who saw it.

And she flung the newspaper down and screamed as no one had ever screamed before or since up on this hill. Olof heard it, presumably lying on his sofa sucking sugar lumps, and he himself, Hadar, heard it as he stood painting over stone chips on his car, and they both dropped what they were doing and rushed off to where the embankment was being built. They could see at once that there had been a terrible accident – something had clearly happened to the boy.

They arrived simultaneously at the hoist and the embankment and the boy, and Olof shouted over and over again, "He's mine, don't touch him! He's mine! Don't you touch him!"

Which was exactly what he, Hadar, had been intending to shout.

Because he could think of nothing more unnatural and abhorrent than for Olof to be the one to free the boy from the chain.

But so conceited and self-absorbed was Olof that he wouldn't let him, Hadar, take the simple action that was so imperative!

The fact was that if anybody had the right to save the boy, to free him and take him in his arms, it was himself, Hadar!

But in his heart of hearts Olof must have simply wanted him dead and buried so that he could be sure where he had him, so that he would never again go to his rightful father and play the guitar.

So he had to overpower and subdue Olof before he could take action to rescue his son.

"But was he still alive?" she asked.

"Oh yes," said Hadar, "he was alive and kicking and waving his arms. And Minna was screaming."

They had thrown themselves at one another up on the embankment, Olof and himself, and wrestled with one another and tried to beat one another to the ground with their fists and feet; they had butted each other like two bull calves and clawed at each other with whichever hand happened to be free, and they had screamed at each other how much they loved the boy.

And in the end they knocked each other down and rolled and tumbled back and forth, with sometimes Olof having the advantage, sometimes Hadar.

Even in those days Olof's body was like a fattened pig ready for slaughter, said Hadar, and he would never forget the revolting odour of vanilla chocolate creams from his mouth.

But finally Hadar had managed to pin Olof beneath him, he had pressed his face into the ground and twisted his arms up behind his back, so that the only thing Olof could do was to jerk and twitch. Thus it was conclusively decided which of them had the sole right to save the boy's life.

Then he, Hadar, became aware that Minna had stopped screaming. And when he sat up and looked at the boy, he saw that he too had stopped, that he was not kicking and waving his arms any more, and he and Minna had helped each other take him down, and Minna had fetched a sheet and they had laid him on the grass.

And all that, he pointed out to her, was without any dimension in time. It neither progressed, nor did it have any beginning, middle or end. It just happened. It was a ghastly event, and Olof had caused it; and most significantly, it had no conclusion.

"Now I need another tablet," Hadar said. "No, not one but two tablets."

When she came back with the tablets and a few spoonfuls of water in a coffee cup he had already fallen asleep.

Her working days were becoming longer and harder. But she was still writing, and she said to Olof, "I'll soon have used up my writing paper; then the book will be finished and I'll be on my way."

"But you'll let him die, at least?"

"Who?"

"That Christopher you're writing about."

"I don't know," she replied. "His death isn't especially important."

"But a book isn't finished until the characters are dead, is it?" he said.

"Hadar's going to die first," she said. "He's going to die before I've finished with St Christopher."

"Hadar won't be first," said Olof. "It was the boy who was first. And then Minna."

"I know," she said. "He's told me everything. Hadar."

"Everything?" said Olof. "Everything?"

Yes, she assumed he had told her everything. She had no reason to distrust Hadar any more than anyone else.

But in that case Olof had to put her right.

It was ridiculous to think that Hadar would have told her everything! After all, in this affair he was nothing but a murderer! Would he have told her how he killed the boy? How he had knocked him, Olof, to the ground so that he was in no position to save the boy's life – the boy had been hanging from a chain – how he had sat on him and held him down, despite the fact that he, Hadar, was actually weaker and lighter. But malevolence and evil had given him a strength that was not of this world. He, Hadar, had set about him with such violence that he shook, and his sweat had poured down on to his, Olof's, head and neck and into his mouth. And Hadar had done this because he knew full well that it was only he, Olof, who really loved the boy. Yes, his sole right to the boy was so obvious and inviolable that he could never have allowed Hadar so much as to touch him, not even now when he was hanging from the chain and flailing with his arms and legs in his struggle for life.

When they had taken the boy down, while Minna was wrapping him in a sheet, he had had to go off to one side to be sick. He had vomited into the newly dug ditch. It was Hadar's sweat that had got into his mouth that he had to spew up, or rather the salt, the unbearable salty taste.

Had Hadar – that was what he really wanted to know – had Hadar told her all that?

Not exactly like that, she said, not exactly.

But to begin with, before Hadar drowned him in his sweat, while he was still able to fight in his attempt to come to the boy's aid, he had had a wonderful taste in his mouth, a taste that came from within himself and that quite simply represented the boy. He had never been able to forget it since.

"And what about Minna?" she asked.

"You can ask Hadar about that," said Olof. "Hadar knows everything. Hadar tells nothing but the truth."

Green grass was starting to spring up around the stone plinth of Hadar's house. She picked some and laid it in the palm of her hand and carried it in to him.

"What do I want grass for?" he asked.

"It's the first of the year," she said. "It smells so green."

But he was not interested in grass. Grass was always the same, it came and went, the grass of his youth was no different from the grass now, towards the end of his days. One sort of grass was indistinguishable from another: the domestic grass round his house was exactly the same as the wild grass in the forest. Grass had various uses, but it had no qualities to raise it above the ordinary and give it any real significance. He had cut and raked and hung grass to dry, he had had it in his shoes and got it inside his shirt, he had relieved himself in it and made a ball of it and rubbed himself clean with it. He had had enough of grass, he had bade farewell to grass, he never wanted to see any again.

"It was just a thought," she said.

But he had objections even to that: she should not think this, that and the other, not about grass nor about him himself nor about Olof for that matter or existence in general. All his life he had avoided believing anything at all. Believing was the same as guessing or imagining or suspecting or at worst lying or telling untruths. Now Olof, he was a believer. Olof believed in God, so He definitely could not exist. Olof thought he would live for ever, so he would evaporate and vaporise like a drop of water on a fire.

"Either you know something," he said, "or you don't."

"Olof says I should ask you about Minna," she said. "And what became of her."

He paused for a moment to concentrate.

"I think she simply disappeared," he said. "I think she went off. I think something happened to her. I think she went to someone else. Sometimes I've thought that she was still here and was hiding."

"But Olof knows?" she said.

"Oh yes. He knows. Olof knows."

Then in conclusion he reverted to the subject of grass, or rather to those near relations of grass, leaves.

"Now leaves," he said, "they're something quite different."

Olof was drying up. However much he scraped at his chest with the teaspoon not a drop issued forth; the pimples were shrinking and disappearing, leaving only yellowish red scabs.

"Like flower buds," Olof said.

But it worried him that he would no longer have recourse to this unexpected supplement to his diet. There was probably no better nourishment. Yet at the same time the disappearance of the pustules could be regarded as a sign of improved health, and maybe it was that very juice that had almost cured him.

The boils had probably been a trick his body had thought up in self-defence. He would like to think his body was as cunning as he was himself. Cunning was the key to survival. Cunning cooperation with your own body was vital.

What had also sometimes occurred to him was one ultimate and decisive act of cunning that would far surpass anything Hadar could possibly conceive: a feigned death.

Hadar would never be capable of carrying out a perfect feigned death. He was too impatient; he lacked the ability to shut out the world and withdraw into himself.

It was simply a matter of closing your eyes and holding your breath. He had practised for short moments now and again. He knew he had the ability to do it.

Feigned death was like suppressed laughter or like our invisible digestion of food. With a feigned death he would be able to outsmart Hadar.

But anyone dying a feigned death had to have a helper and ally, otherwise you could be buried alive by mistake, and then the feigned death would be in vain. Alone, the sham corpse would have no chance. Yes, Hadar would have him buried even if he rose up in the coffin and let the whole world witness the deception.

If only he had someone, if he had had Minna, then he could have led Hadar a merry dance with his feigned death!

"Hadar thinks you have Minna concealed here in the house," she said.

At that he lay in silence for a long time. He said no more about feigned death, and from his throat there came a hacking cough. Then he said, "So that's what Hadar has believed all these years!"

"I don't know," she said. "But that's what he believes now."

"I've always wanted to know," he said, "what Hadar thought about Minna. What a puzzle it must have been for him! How he must have fretted!"

Spittle was running out of the corners of his mouth as he spoke, and the pillow-case was getting spotted and stained. It needed washing again already.

"Hadar is worried," she said. "He worries about everything and everyone."

"You mustn't say a word to him," Olof said. "Not a word to Hadar!"

"What mustn't I say?"

"About Minna," he said. "What I'm going to tell you now."

"I don't know what you're going to tell me about Minna," she said. "And Hadar no longer hears me. He just talks to himself."

"No one knows it except me," said Olof. "No one must

know. If you tell Hadar, about the summer of fifty-nine, about Minna, I won't have the upper hand any more."

"Neither of you has the upper hand," she said. "Neither you nor Hadar."

"Then you would never be able to come to see me again," he said. "I would be done with you."

"Whenever I hear about anything," she said, "I always forget it straight away."

"You remember Minna," he said. "You remember what she looked like. You remember how slim and slight she was. You remember how she used to wash her hair in the rainwater barrel and her hair was like bleached flax."

"I can't remember her. I've never seen her."

"But you must recall," Olof said, "how white her skin was and how she used to screw up her eyes against the light, and you remember her voice and her lips that were really red, and you remember the cakes she used to bake and the porridge she used to make."

"Yes," she said. "I remember."

"But the last time you saw Minna," he said, "you didn't know anything."

"No, nothing."

"That was just the way she was."

"Yes. That was the way she was."

When they got home again after burying the boy – and this was what she must never tell Hadar – when he and Minna got home, when he had changed his trousers and jacket and shirt, Minna had carried the wicker chair outside and sat down at the back of the house, beneath the kitchen window, the wicker chair from the bedroom. She had sat right in the full sun. She had undone her dress to catch the sun and taken off the glasses that were meant to protect her from the sunlight. And there she sat, that was all she did, she sat.

She moved the chair round to follow the sun. And she didn't even close her eyes. And the summer of fifty-nine was nothing but sunshine, sun all day and all night.

"You can't take the sun, Minna," he had said. "You'll come out in a rash. The sun will be the death of you. You know that, you're made for the shade and indoors."

But she had not answered him. She seemed not to hear him, she just shifted her position a little in the chair.

"We ought at least to have a little funeral feast," he had said. "Just you and me, a few cakes and a tart and some raspberry juice."

But it hadn't helped, nothing had helped.

He had stood on tiptoe to make himself tall and solemnly besought her to go inside with him. He had abased himself on the ground in front of her, on the grass that was withering in the heat of the sun. And all the time he had been spitting out the sweet mucus and watery blood.

But it was as if she could not see him.

"Dear little Minna," he had said, "you shouldn't just think of yourself. I'm famished; someone ought to get the meal."

Even then, that first evening, she had felt hot when he put his hand on her, as if she had a high fever, and her skin had been blotchy as if it were beginning to disintegrate. She had also refused to come in and go to bed. When he undressed and went to bed she was sitting on the north side of the house, with the sun still shining on her.

Two more days passed in the same way. She had followed the sun and he had stayed almost constantly at her side in the deepest despair and half starving. At times he had even stood right in front of her to provide shade. Once he had taken hold of her to lift her up and carry her in. "We still have each other, Minna," he had said, "if you abandon me I won't be able to survive!"

At that point she interrupted him and said, "But you have survived after all."

"Yes," he said. "I've been managing better and better. And I'll soon be on my feet again after this little illness. That's the ineffable grace of God."

When he had tried to take hold of her and lift her up and carry her indoors, she had lunged out and scratched at his cheeks with her nails so that he had to release her and go and wash off the blood in the water bucket.

He had taken the ladle outside and poured water over her to cool her down. Her eyelids had puffed up over her eyes, which might have been a relief for her: she could never bear to see the sunshine. And her hair had started falling out, the way the hairs fall from cotton-grass. Her cheeks and her chin and neck had become red and swollen, and little cracks were opening up in her skin.

"But you're not to breathe a word to Hadar!"

"No, not a word."

When he came out to her on the morning of the fourth day she was dead. She had let the sun take her. She was sitting dead in the wicker chair. She looked beautiful, but in a different and rounder way than before. He could never understand what had got into her, what she had really intended, what madness had overtaken her. Perhaps she had simply wanted to see whether she could grow accustomed to the sun.

"And Hadar?" she asked.

Hadar? No, none of this was anything to do with Hadar. Only that he bore the entire responsibility for what had happened, the whole thing was his fault – but apart from that it was nothing to do with him.

When they arrived back home after burying the boy, he and Minna, the ditch had been filled in. Hadar had done it, and it was as if the boy had never existed. And that was what he had said to Minna: all Hadar wants to do is to obliterate and extinguish everything.

Then they had seen Hadar rushing off in the car. Minna was already sitting outside in the wicker chair, on the south side of the house, so she probably didn't see anything, but she must have heard the engine roaring and the wheels skidding on the gravel. Hadar had rushed off at tremendous speed, and the dust from the road had blown right over to their house. It was as if he were impelled by something, no doubt his conscience.

So there Minna had sat. And there he had stood. He who could understand Minna so well, he who knew her inside out!

"Can you comprehend it?" he asked. "Does it make any sense to you?"

"It's time for me to go," she said. "I must get Hadar ready for the night."

Hadar had stayed away for several days. He, Olof, had almost begun to hope that he would never return.

So when Minna was dead he was able to take her in to the village without Hadar knowing anything about it. He took her there and had her buried as she was. It was rather like a family grave, her and the boy.

"If you say as much as a word to Hadar, a single word about Minna, you'll see no more of me!"

And she reassured him again, "I won't ever say a thing."

"You went away," she said to Hadar. "When your son that you had with Minna was dead, that summer of fifty-nine, didn't you go away?"

"I've never gone away," he said. "You'd have to be out of your mind to leave here."

"But you got in your car and drove off?"

No, he couldn't remember having done that. No, he had never gone away. As far as he could remember. It had never been in his nature to go away.

Going away from here had always seemed to him akin to dying.

Anyone who goes away has to return in the end, and that is probably the worst part of it, considerably worse than going away. A person who returns brings with him nothing but disappointment and regret, grief and heartache.

"Olof says you did. And you stayed away for a good many days."

"So he remembers me?" Hadar said. "He mentioned me by name?"

"Yes," she said. "He remembers you. He remembers you all the time."

"When I still counted myself among the living," Hadar said, "I often used to remember all sorts of things myself."

And his memory was still unimpaired, he could assure her. He could still bring it back to life whenever he wanted to. Such as now in the case of this speedy departure after the loss of his son. When Olof had caused his death. Now that she mentioned it.

If she was really interested he could remember that day very well, and having indeed gone away, in a manner of speaking. It had not been any grand or momentous departure, he had just quietly and unobtrusively slipped away. It had been a necessity for him. He had been struck by the realisation that he would never again share his herring and bacon with anybody. Never again would anybody step through his door and say, "Have you got a piece of bacon, Hadar?" Or, "Any chance of half a herring?"

Nobody would sit opposite him at the table boning a herring or spreading butter on bread and eating. And people have to have somebody to eat with now and again. Salt bacon and herring. So he had simply gone away.

But it was not anything particularly worth remembering. He had had a vague idea that he would find someone, that he would come across someone, not any special person but just someone, anyone really.

If she insisted he could bring to mind all the little roads he had driven along, the hill where his radiator had started to overheat, the places he had stayed the night, the villages he had driven through without being able to bring himself to step on the brake, the cheese and sausage that had come to an end and finally forced him to go back home again. So he had returned empty-handed, and if she so wished he could remember that too. It was as simple as that.

But what was the point of recalling all these futile things? If she thought it absolutely necessary he could remember it by all means, but he would be grateful if he could leave his memory undisturbed, if, in a word, he could forget it. He would rather not have to wear out his memory unnecessarily.

"I'm not trying to force you into anything," she said.

He might perhaps add – and this did not involve any reliance on his memory – that this modest excursion in fifty-nine, the time when he in a sense went away, had only now reached its final conclusion when he so very recently drove into the village and fetched her here so that she could write her book in peace and quiet.

For the first part of her stay, a long time ago, before the cancer had completely robbed him of his enjoyment of food, they had certainly sat across the table from one another eating this and that together.

Now she had one hundred and fifty closely written pages. It was almost enough. It was at least a start. There were provisional notes in the margin about chapter divisions and new paragraphs. There too were the inevitable question marks, exclamation marks and dashes. And hastily scrawled words like unnecessary! unclear! superficial! stupid!

"I'm far from satisfied," she told Hadar. "I'm never satisfied."

"You say yourself that nobody reads your books," Hadar replied. "So it doesn't much matter, I suppose."

"Well, somebody might," she said.

"I dreamt about your St Christopher last night," he said. "I saw him from behind. I saw him running up the hill. And I saw you racing after him, with your hair streaming out behind you. Then I saw you stumble and fall and him get away from you."

"Yes," she said. "Yes, that's what it's like."

*

"You were right," she said to Hadar. "About Minna. She went away. She left Olof, and went off with what little she possessed in a suitcase."

"Yes," said Hadar, "that's what I thought, that's what I've always believed. She was never happy with Olof. He had become a real torment to her."

"And Olof didn't know anything," she said. "One morning the bed was empty and she was gone. She hadn't said a word to him. He didn't know where she was or what had happened to her for many years."

"Ah," said Hadar, "she was the cleverest one of us. She had no choice. What else could she do?"

"She could have come here," she said. "To you."

"Why should she have done that? There was no future for her with me."

"But a few years ago," she said, "he heard what had happened to her and where she had gone."

"Fancy no one saying anything to me," said Hadar.

"She's in one of the towns out on the coast, she's getting on well, and everything turned out for the best for her."

"That's what I always thought," said Hadar. "Things will probably work out all right for Minna, I thought."

"She found a job as a housekeeper," she continued. "With a timber merchant. Called Lundberg."

"I think I've heard of him," said Hadar.

"And she's borne him two sons. They're grown up now. One of them's a lawyer and living in Stockholm."

"And Olof told you all this?"

"Yes. Olof told me."

"A lawyer," Hadar said. "In Stockholm. Ah, time goes so fast we'll never understand it."

"And the doctors have treated Minna," she said. "They've found a drug that has given her as much colour as a person could want. Her hair and eyebrows are chestnut brown and in the summer she gets freckled and sunburnt. She looks like a normal woman."

"Just like everyone else?" said Hadar.

"Yes," she said. "Like everyone else."

"Well," said Hadar, "well, then I wouldn't have wanted her in any case."

The smooth skin on Olof's neck and chins had begun to wrinkle. Perhaps he was getting thinner. Lifting the upper part of his body to dry the sweat on his back was no longer such heavy work. He said so himself: "Either I'm wasting away or else I'll soon be running around on Sedgemarsh Meadow digging up bumblebee nests."

It was a day when thick black clouds had gathered over the furthest peaks, hiding the sun, so that daylight never really seemed to break through.

After she had put everything out for him that he might need for the night she sat down for a moment on the chair by the door.

"Hadar is dead," she told him.

He unfolded his hands that were clasped across his chest and raised them to his face so that they covered his cheeks and eyes but not his mouth.

"What did you say?" he exclaimed.

"Hadar is dead," she replied. And she repeated it, "Hadar is dead now."

When he asked her a second time she did not answer.

He heaved several deep sighs, his long-drawn-out breaths

causing a sibilant wheezing from his throat and chest.

"Did he have a difficult time?" he asked.

"Yes," she said, "very difficult. I've never seen a person suffer so much. He was moaning and groaning and tossing about for two days and nights. At the end I could hardly recognise him any more."

After a while Olof started talking about what this meant: that he was left standing, or rather lying, as victor, that God had finally intervened after all and put everything to rights.

No one would be sorry that Hadar was dead; it was perfectly proper of him to be dead, and no one would miss him. Not even in life had he ever been missed; on the contrary, wherever he happened to be he had been superfluous, and not just a superfluous but also a pernicious presence.

In his heart of hearts he, Olof, had always thought it would end like this.

Admittedly he had sometimes been tormented by doubt, but his belief had given him the strength to hold on. After this no one could say that he lacked perseverance, that he was not the stronger and better man. This was quite simply a blessing, that was what it was. And retribution. A blessing and retribution.

For himself, Olof, it was an almost incomprehensible triumph – it was the greatest success in his life. He only wished he had someone to share his joy and satisfaction with, his parents or Minna or the boy or anybody.

Tonight he would stay awake until dawn and enjoy the sweet feeling of victory.

As she stood up and left he was still talking, to himself

and to her and to Hadar and to the whole world. The bank of black cloud had come nearer and now hung over the lake. It had started snowing again.

All Hadar needed for the night was a couple of glasses of water and his painkillers. She put them on the chair for him.

"Nothing else?" she asked.

"What else could there be?" he said.

Then she said, "When I went over to Olof's cottage today I found him dead."

"Now you're lying," said Hadar. "Now you're lying to me."

"Why should I lie? You would notice it straight away if I lied."

"I think," said Hadar, "that he's been dead a long time, but you haven't wanted to tell me. You thought I wouldn't be able to bear to hear it. You thought that if he, Hadar, finds out that Olof is dead, he'll die himself."

"He was dead when I got there," she said. "I closed his eyes. And his mouth."

"I can bear to hear it," said Hadar. "I can bear anything. But if Olof had lived, he wouldn't have been able to bear hearing that I was dead."

That had been the crucial difference between him and Olof, that he had been able to bear things. Olof had been weak and thin-skinned and fastidious. Olof always had to have everything he set eyes on, whereas he, Hadar, had learnt to do without.

He, Hadar, had actually been the one his mother had wanted, that she had been so fond of, but Olof had come and pushed him away from her breast. Olof had had the sweet taste of mother's milk on his tongue all his life. He had always been sucking and slurping. When his mother died he had unbuttoned her nightdress to put her nipple in his mouth one last time. And that was all he had managed to do with Minna, just sucking her in one place or another.

He, Hadar, had never asked for anything for himself, he had borne all his trials and kept himself going by his own strength. He had never demanded any pleasure or consolation, he had always shared what he had, it was a simple as that. He could probably even bear to hear how Olof had suffered on his deathbed, in his loneliness.

"I wasn't there," she said. "I just found him."

"I know," said Hadar, "but even so."

"His tongue was dark blue and sticking out between his lips," she said. "And his cheeks were suffused with blood and there was a pattern of black streaks all over his skin."

"I can well believe it," said Hadar. "I can see him in my mind's eye."

If what she was saying were true – and he could just as easily imagine otherwise – if Olof really were dead, then his own existence was changed fundamentally forthwith. And since she had described Olof in death in such detail and in so lifelike a manner, he had to believe her.

Inasmuch as Olof had passed away, in that case, then, he supposed that from today he had become his heir.

And since Olof could no longer steal everything from him, it was time for him to start living properly, to help himself to things, to look forward and make plans for the future, make arrangements for this and that. Present existence was not for ever, life was not like a locked room or a sheepfold with no way out; no, it was full of other avenues and unforeseen possibilities. There were no restrictions or limits to what might happen now.

Admittedly, some might think – as indeed might she – that he had come too far in his life for such ideas to have any meaning. But of all earthly substances time was the most supple and pliant. You always have the time you need; at every moment you have exactly the time you need.

"I have time," he said. "Time is what I have."

He had been thinking for ages that he would knock down Olof's house and build himself a sauna. But now he might even consider letting it stand. He could carry out improvements, repair the roof and put in a cooking stove and hang a lamp in the porch. The house was actually not uninhabitable, and he could get himself some neighbours. In the winters to come, when it was dark and he was without company, he would be able to stand at his own window and see the light in the windows below and the sparks from the chimney.

"I've got a few more lines to write," she said.

"Of course," he said, "you go on up. I'll be fine. I can manage all right now."

When she came down in the morning the sofa was empty. There was no sign of Hadar. The bucket was in its place, the water in the glasses had been drunk, but his painkillers were still untouched on the chair, and the wooden doll lay on the windowsill. It looked as if he had left everything suddenly, as if he had gone away in a great hurry or as if someone had unexpectedly come and fetched him.

"Hadar?" she said. "Hadar?"

She went to the window and looked out. Olof's house was

barely visible and the forest and the lake were completely hidden by their covering of snow.

Then she turned round and saw him.

There he was.

He was finally demonstrating, even exemplifying, how the special contraption on the wall should be used. It was in perfect working order.

Anyone who managed, or had the strength, to die standing up in the special contraption would for some considerable time, perhaps for ever, have the upper hand over anyone who listlessly and passively let himself die lying down. Perhaps not in a strictly physical sense, but spiritually, and in terms of human conduct.

His outstretched arms, his forehead, his chest and knees were pressed against the rough branches that were fixed to the wall with nails, screws and bolts. When she touched him she could feel that he was nearly cold. He was dead, but he was standing on his feet, ridiculous yet dignified.

His eyes were already closed, so she did not need to do it. She cut a strip from his pillow case and bound up his jaw, tying the knot in a full upstanding bow on the top of his head.

When she had fetched the newspaper and made a fire in the stove she sat down on the sofa, by the arm where he always used to rest his feet, and looked at him. She was chewing at a hunk of dry bread that she had taken from the pantry.

Then she went upstairs to the little writing table by the window and completed the sentence she had left half-finished the evening before.

*

She released him from the contraption, not without difficulty, since he had now begun to stiffen. Then she took him in her arms and carried him out of the door, heaving him up on to her shoulders when she was outside on the steps. He felt practically weightless.

Her feet kept slipping on the soft snow, though she walked with splayed legs and bent slightly forward so as not to drop him. Once or twice she nearly fell.

But Hadar soon started getting heavier, much heavier. His feet bumped against her right knee, his head and neck chafed against the inside of her left elbow. Her stride became more halting, her footsteps shorter, her breath laboured and uneven, and she had to keep stopping to rest. "My God, Hadar!" she said. "My God!"

Where the snow had piled up in drifts she had to wade and shuffle through them. His hipbone was digging into the vertebrae of her neck, cramp in her long slim fingers forced her to keep shifting her grip, and she tried to stretch out her left arm that had gone numb. The burden that had so soon and so surprisingly almost become too much for her was weighing down on her pelvis so heavily that she was forced to bend further and further forward. "Hadar," she sputtered, "I'm not going to make it."

But she got there in the end, stumbled up the steps, pushed open the door and went into the hall.

When she kicked at the kitchen door she received no reply. Using Hadar's head, she managed to push the handle down and open the door enough to squeeze through sideways.

"Olof," she said, "I've brought Hadar."

But he did not answer.

With Hadar still over her shoulders she crossed to the

sofa where Olof lay with his hands clasped under his chin. She leant over a bit more and put her ear to his chest, listening just above his armpit and then further down, by his breastbone, but there was absolute silence. He was as dead as Hadar, no more and no less.

His nose was slightly more prominent than in life and his cheeks had sunk in; there was a smile on his face. A white scummy blob oozed from the corner of his mouth. It could have been something he was trying to eat, but it could equally well have been something that came from inside him. Some sort of fluid was leaking from Hadar and soaking into her back.

She straightened up, turned round and let Hadar fall on to the sofa, dropping him next to Olof or on top of him.

Then she stood there for a while rubbing her back and trying to massage her neck and shoulders. She also took a few moments to have a good look at the two brothers. Her legs were trembling.

Hadar's face was uppermost, his cheek resting against Olof's. His outstretched, slightly bent left arm was lying across Olof's clasped hands, and his fingertips were brushing Olof's ear. His body was curved up against Olof's distended belly, his stiffly extended legs pressing up against Olof's thighs and knees. Olof's head had moved slightly along the pillow, making Hadar's repose more comfortable.

Despite their rigidity they both looked natural and relaxed, even content, in their brotherly embrace.

The snowplough would be coming that evening or during the night. Then she would be on her way exactly as she had intended. She would walk up to the road and hail it, and would ride in the cab to the village.

The structure of the sentence left over from the night before, the one she had completed that morning, was probably still not quite right. Although St Christopher's life may seem magnificent and poignant, she had written, perhaps even noble and beautiful, it also had an element of rather absurd formlessness and meaninglessness, that peculiar but by no means uncommon futility that is the inevitable result of such morbidly heightened expectations, of that desire, exaggerated to the point of obsession, for structure and meaning; the lack of personal meaning and significance finds its strongest expression in a fatal diminution of vitality, a wilful indifference to life, to simple everyday life in its varied and splendid fullness, and its rich diversity is restricted and reduced to the most incontestable and glaring uniformity.

She ought to divide it up. One sentence about meaninglessness and one sentence about indifference would be better. Then she would be able to move on.